It's My Life

It's My Life

By

EVIE BROOKS

FLO'S PRODUCTIONS PUBLISHING SERVICE
An Affiliate of Writers & Self Publishers Association

WSPA
Writers and Self Publisher's Association
Genesee County

First Published by Flo's Productions
Website: www.flosproductions.biz
Email: flosproductions@comcast.net or writersandselfpublishers@yahoo.com
For more information on publishing call: (810) 334-2837

Manuscript and Project by Evie Brooks
Front and Back cover Illustrations by Flo's Productions
Inside author's photograph provided by Evie Brooks

ISBN 0-9769645-8-9

Printed in the United States of America

DEDICATED

to

John

John II

Jessica

Ruby, Dericco and Manvel

Also in loving memory of

Naomi Huddleston,

and Quincey C. Loyd

FROM THE PUBLISHER

My first initial meeting with Author Evie Brooks was very exciting. Within a few moments of meeting her, we hit it right off. I found her to be quite an interesting lady. Evie is very shy by nature. Although, she is quite shy she has no problem expressing what she wants. When I read through the first few pages of *It's My Life* I was hooked on what was going to happen to the main character (Danielle). Publishing *It's My Life* was going to be my first Romance publication. Therefore, I was not only moved by working closely with the author to get the novel published; I was determined to make sure it was going to be a very exciting novel for the readers. I knew some of the contents would be shocking. I was certainly amazed with the outcome of the story while I was editing *It's My Life*. I found myself many times getting so involved with the characters life. Some of the other works I've published were more inspirational pieces. However, I was willing to take a chance on some of my critics. I love adventure, suspence, excitement and stories that are challenging. *It's My Life* was filled with all of these attributes and more. I want to thank Evie for writing such a wonder love story.

Evie you are a breath of fresh air. I am grateful that you chose Flo's Productions to suite your publishing needs. I certainly look forward to working with you to publish more novels in the future. God Bless you in all your future endeavors.

Sincerely,
Florence J. Dyer
Author/Publisher/Designer
President/CEO of Flo's Productions

TABLE OF CONTENTS

FORWARD

It's My Life is about a young impressionable sheltered teenage girl named Danielle. She has been sheltered through a religious upbringing enforced upon her by an overbearing mother. Towards the end of her senior year in high school, she discovers a lot of the things her mom shielded her from were not what she wanted for herself. In fact, she wanted to do away with a lot of things she was indoctrinated to believe. Danielle gradually develops a new set of her own beliefs. In discovering her own emancipation she decides to take on a whole new set of values to live by. She becomes acquainted with her history teacher. The two of them develop a very torrid love affair. Through the affair Danielle discovers a lot about men. Through her hurt, and disappointments she learns that she will survive.

It's My Life is filled with romance, deception, lies, betrayal and suspense. Author Evie Brooks keeps her readers on the edge of their seats wondering about Danielle's next discovery. Her life is filled with drama, intrigue and mystery. The choices she makes will surprise the reader. Young Danielle's life begins with her being a young innocent curious sheltered teenager who ultimately matures into a self assured young woman.

Any woman that has gained their independence can identify with Danielle. It is nothing like being able to pay your own way. She loves being able to stand on her own two feet. Danielle is a model for every woman who has been in an abusive or addictive relationship. She lets us know that there is still a prince charming around every dark cloud. *It's My Life* is an awesome love story.

Florence J. Dyer

Chapter One: Last Weeks of High School

Today is the end of May. It is a beautiful sunny day just a bit too hot and humid. I am glad this is my last day of school. Thank God, it is just a half a day of school because it is too hot to be sitting in a stifling classroom taking final exams. I can think of other things I'd rather do, than be in school.

Hooray! Graduation is in two weeks-- I cannot wait. No more studying, and I will not have to deal with those crazy kids and the mean teachers who do not want to be at school anyways-- all they want is their paycheck. I am not looking forwarded to being at home either.

I always thought that I could not wait to be out of school, but I did not think of how it would be living with my parents twenty-four/ seven. At least my dad has a job to go to but my mom was always fussing at me about cleaning the house. I had to clean my bedroom, all three bathrooms, the kitchen, and the family room.

I have three brothers-- what is their purpose for living. Mom never makes them clean up! I guess the boys just figure housework is a girl's job. Our house cannot get any cleaner-- you can already eat off of our floors.

I know I am going to hate being out of school because my parents are so strict; I can't go anywhere for heaven's sake, I can't even go and visit my next-door neighbors. How crazy is that? Why are my parents so strict? My best friend Kim is afraid to come over to my house because she hates to hear my mom fuss at me so much. My parents are Christians, so why can't they trust me? I cannot go anywhere unless they are with me. Most of the time my younger brother David has to go along with me. Yeah, I already know that being at home with my mom is going to be torture for me. My only hope is to find a job just to keep my sanity.

The school bell rings. I hurry up to say good-bye to the people I am going to miss. On my way home from school, I wonder what I am going to do with my life. I do not have any special skills and I do not have any hobbies, since my parent's religion thinks it is a sin to have fun-- going bowling, skating, or anything that has to do with fun. Hell, I could not go to my own prom-- not to mention, I never went to a basketball game or football game. Why my parents and other church folks thought that any of these things could be a sin, I do not know. I did not see it anywhere in the bible that having fun was a sin.

I cannot wait to get out of my parents' house and get a place of my own. One thing is for sure I will not be going to church anymore. I will not let those so call church folks tell me how to live my life. I do not know why none of my teachers or counselors help guide me or help me decide-- what I wanted to do, when I finished school? I guess I cannot blame them completely because my parents did not help me at all. I should take some of the blame myself because I should have had an idea of what I wanted to be when I got out of high school.

When I got home from school, my mom wanted me to go to the grocery store and pick up a few things for dinner. I ask my mom, "can I relax and catch my breath, since I just walked home from school," and my mom said yes. Then she begins to tell me about how she uses to walk miles and miles to the store with holes in her shoes. Here we go again. I was tired of hearing the same story over and over again. I said, "okay mom I am ready to go to the store." I thought to myself, I do not want to hear that same old story again.

On the way to the store, I must have walked about fifteen houses down; when I turned the corner and heard someone on the porch calling my name. I turned around slowly to see who was calling my name. In what I thought was a very sexy and masculine tone. The voice sounded very familiar to me but no, it could not be who I think it is. As I turned around to see who it was, it indeed was my history teacher.

As I walked toward him, I hoped he did not see how much I was sweating. It was not just from the heat outside but I have had a crush on Mr. Wax for the past three years.

I had no idea that he lived there as many times as I passed by this house.

Mr. Wax has a nice physique, he is tall, and has a dark complexion, he is so fine. He has the most beautiful brown eyes; he has a smile that just would not quit with those sexy dimples. His voice was so soothing, it would make you melt.

In his class, it is hard to concentrate on the assignments because I would be fantasizing about him. I would think about us kissing and other things. I am sure the other girls in the class felt the same way I did, because my best friend and I would always talk about him and how we looked forward to seeing him everyday. He made our day just by looking at him. When the female teachers talk to him, they would have a big grin on their faces too. I know they also wanted to get with him.

Naturally, when he called my name I was wondering what he wanted with me. I was not a popular girl in school. I was quiet and shy. I weighed about hundred and twenty-five pounds. I was about 5'6'. I had long black hair hanging downs my back. I had a lot of booty with no breast.

I am curious to hear what he has to say to me. Mr. Wax invited me into his house and at first, I was scared to go inside of his house but since he is one of my teachers; I decided it would be okay. I am sure that he is not going to hurt me or anything besides it is hot out here and I want to cool off anyways.

He asked me to have a seat, and I saw a brown leather chair that really looked comfortable. The chair was designed to seat only one person. As I walked over to sit in the chair, he beat me to it first. It was as if he was reading my mind. Since he took the chair I sat on the love seat. I was still a little nervous and hoped he would not come and sit next to me.

He asked me what I plan on doing with my life, since school is almost over. I said, I did not know since I do not have any special skills. My parents already told me that going to college is not an option. They had no left money after sending my three brothers to college.

He asked me, if I have a boyfriend. I looked at him and laughed. Then said, you must be kidding, no boy in this neighborhood would be crazy enough to date me. They all know how mean my parents are. Besides that, my brothers would kill anybody who tried to talk to me. I could only imagine what they would do to a guy who tried to date me.

He then asked me, if I ever been kissed before? I said yes of course. "Was he a good kisser?" Mr. Wax asked. I told him, I guess I really do not remember it too much, because I was in the seventh grade. I ask him, if he remembered his first kiss? He said yes, but it was nothing to brag about.

He then moved from his chair and sat next to me on the love seat. I became even more nervous. I felt my body getting hot all over and not from the heat outside. I felt butterflies in my stomach. It became hard to breath. As he moved closer, I could feel the electricity from his body heating up my body. He took my right hand and held it in his hand. He told me that he had been dreaming about me since the first day of class. What he said next really shocked me. He said, one day I wore a white blouse and a tight orange skirt with my legs crossed. When I uncrossed my legs he saw my orange panties. He said, it turned him on and he had a hard on until the end of class.

After he told the story, he eased over even closer to me. He then leaned over and kissed me. At first I thought about pulling away. Nevertheless, he was turning me on. I did not want to stop; besides I was anxiously awaiting to feel his lips on my lips. It felt great. I wanted the kiss to last forever. I hoped he was enjoying the kiss as much as I was enjoying it.

We came up for air, then started back kissing. It was so good. I wanted to stay stuck to his lips but the stupid phone rung. I held him close to me hoping that he would not stop kissing me, but he said that he had to answer it. He was expecting an important call. It seemed like he is on the phone a long time but actually it was just a couple of minutes. When he got off the phone he sat back down next to me. He asked where did he leave off? We begin to kiss again, and of course, it felt as good as before.

He stood up and pulled me close to him. We begin to slow dance, I told him that I was not a good dancer. Also, that I had never danced before. He said, that is okay because he was an excellent dancer and he pulled me even closer to him. He is right he is an excellent dancer. I felt his heart beating fast. Then I felt his penis getting hard. I still did not push him away even though I knew what might be happening next. We slowly danced down the hallway to his bedroom and then we dance over to his bed. Then he gently laid me down on his bed and he begins kissing me on my neck. Then he whispered in my ear that he knew that I am a virgin. He said that he would be gentle with me, and that he would not hurt me. At this point, I did not care about anything but to have him inside of me. Once he was inside of me, he seemed to be moaning. He was saying how good it felt to him. All I could feel was pain; I wanted it to end. He was asking me how it felt to me? I pretended like I was enjoying it. The truth was that I wanted him to stop. I thought that the first time I made love the earth was going to shake. I thought it was going to feel so good.

Afterwards we took a shower together. We kissed but nothing else happened. Why do people make a big deal out of having sex? At this point I felt like I should have waited but it's too late for that. The deed is done now.

After I got dressed, I looked at the clock and I begin to freak out. Oh no, I said. I was supposed to be at the grocery store and at home by now. I told Mr. Wax that my mother was going to kill me because she knows that it does not take an hour and a half to get home.

He calmed me down. He told me that everything was going to be alright. He would drive me to the store and then take me home. I thought about what he said but I told him everything sounds good but he could not drop me off at my house. He said, all right. He would drop me off at the corner. I told him if my mom sees me get out of his car, she would kill me. I hurried into the store and then I returned to his car. Before I got out of his car at the corner from my house, he gave me a kiss. He told me to call him later. I said okay, when I get the chance. Thanks for the ride.

As I walked toward my house, I felt funny. It hurt when I

walked. I wondered if anyone could tell that I just had sex for the first time. It felt like something was stuck in my virgina. I wondered if my mom would be able to tell by the way I walked or the look on my face. I felt like I was a woman now.

When I opened up the back door, my mother was standing there waiting for me to come in. Before I entered into the house, she began to yell at me and threaten to beat my butt. I quickly put the groceries away and I rushed upstairs. After dinner, I cleaned up the kitchen, hurried downstairs, and called Mr. Wax. He asked me if I was okay and did, I get in trouble with my mom? With a sigh of relief, I told him everything was okay.

He told me how much he enjoyed, making love to me. He could not wait to hold me in his arms again and make love to me. He asked when could he see me again and I told him that I did not know because my parents never let me go anywhere but to the store. I knew I could not continue using the store excuse everyday.

He suggested that I sneak out of the house when my parents and brother went to sleep. I am thinking that this is the craziest thing I ever heard. I thought he was crazy for even suggesting this.

A couple of days went by and I was missing him so much. Although, I would talk to him everyday that was not enough. Talking to him was not the same as him holding me or dancing with me. I was not thinking about making love because the last time it hurt too much.

I begin to think about sneaking out of the house because I was missing him so much. I wanted him to hold me close. Then I wondered about how could I sneak out of the house. How could I get up the nerves? Also, I wondered what would happen if I sneak, out of the house? What if my brother caught me; worst of all what if I got caught by my parents? Still I kept thinking about getting enough nerves to sneak out anyways.

Another day has passed. I have not seen him. When I talked to him on the phone, he was telling me how much he missed me and he needed to see me tonight and he encourage me to sneak out of the house and he begin to give me advise of how to sneak out and what time to leave the house.

It is after midnight and I am about to make my move to sneak out. So I could be with Mr. Wax. My first thought was to us the doors. But the doors will make too much noise. So I decided I will have to go out one of the big windows, in the family room on the front of the house. Big shrubby bushes covered the windows. This seemed to be the best idea. Therefore, I opened the window quietly making sure I did not make a sound. After I got outside, I looked around and made sure no one was outside to see me. Then I ran to the corner as fast as I could. When I got to the corner, I slowed down, so that I would not be tired when I got to Mr. Wax's house.

When I got to his house, he was surprise to see me because he did not think I had enough nerves to sneak out of the house. Before I could get into his house good, he begins to kiss me. He told me how much he missed me. He said, that the sex from the last time was so good; he could not wait to get inside of me.

This time he did not slow dance with me. We just went to the bedroom and got busy. This time it felt good it did not hurt, as much. I guess I was more relaxed this time around. This time it felt like an earthquake, I swear the bed and the house was moving. I know earthquakes do not happen in Michigan. But it did in that room.

I figured this was a sign that we were suppose to be together forever. I got in the shower as the water ran over my body I was wondering why the first time didn't feel as good. All I knew is that I wanted to keep having this feeling. This was a great feeling of pleasure I never knew could exist. Now I understood why people made a big deal about sex.

After getting dressed, we went to the living room. We talked about how we need to find a way to be together, without having to sneak out of the house. We did not come up with a solution and it was getting too late, so I had to go home. Mr. Wax walked me to the corner and watched me until I was out of sight.

When I got back to the house I was scared. I looked around outside to make sure no lights was on inside the house. I proceeded with caution into the window. It was dark but I had my little flashlight, which did not throw off a lot of light. It gave off just enough light to see in front of me.

My heart was beating so fast. I knew in order to make it back to my bedroom; I had to be very quite. I tiptoed ever so lightly in front of my parent's bedroom. I was glad that they always kept their door closed. I still could hear my dad snoring. I felt safe now. I thought if they heard me now, I would just say, I was on my way to the bathroom. I had worn my pajamas over to Mr. Wax house just in case my parent would see me in the hallway.

When I laid in the bed, I was so surprised that I really sneaked out of the house. I had to pinch myself to make sure that I was not dreaming.

I didn't know that I had the nerves to do something like that. I soon fell asleep.

From this point on, I continued to sneak out of the house. I would go to Mr. Wax's house at least three times a week. I figure I got sneaking out of the house down to a science. I was not scared anymore.

I went looking for a job today because I needed an excuse to spend more time with him and I do not like the idea of sneaking out of the house anymore.

I got a job finally a couple of days later. I was so happy to get out of the house because my mom was really getting on my last nerves.

The more I worked, the less I saw of Mr. Wax. I begin to meet more guys especially ones around my age but most of them came in the store with their girlfriends.

I slowly begin to lose interest in Mr. Wax but now I was addicted to sex. So I figured he was better than having no man. So I had better stick with him. Every time he called I didn't want to be with him or I didn't feel like sneaking out. So I would make an excuse, about why I couldn't sneak out or why I couldn't talk to him on the phone.

Chapter Two: Graduation Day

There was a two-week break for all graduating seniors. I was really looking forward to saying my final good-byes to the people I have missed for the last two weeks. It was hard to say good-bye because I knew that I probably would never see some of them again. There were certain friends I really missed over the past two weeks. I was wondering what they had been doing since we been out of school? What were they planning on doing with their lives and how many of them were going away to attend college?

Finally it is graduation day. I was especially looking forward to seeing Mr. Wax. I just wanted to see how he would react to seeing me in public. Would he ignore me or will he speak to me? I wanted to see his reaction when he was around the other girls. I wanted to see if he treated any other girl the same way he treated me. Well, when I saw him he walked over to me and gave me a big tight hug and whispered in my ear and said that he needed to see me tonight that it has been too long and he needed to make love to me. So I said okay, I would go over to his house tonight. I must admit, I did not expect him to hug me that tight it really caught me off guard. He did hug a whole lot of girls.

Once again, I sneaked out of the house liked I had done so many times before. The sex was still great, it seemed to be getting better and better as if I was getting addicted to sex. It felt like I needed it more than ever.

When I got to his house, I had to use the bathroom. While I was in there, I heard the doorbell ring.

Who could that be coming over to his house this time of night. I cracked the door open a little bit to see, if I could see or hear who was at the door. I heard a woman voice but I could not hear what they were saying. I looked out of the bathroom window, since it was in the front of the house. I got a glimpse of the woman walking to her car. I recognized the car and who she was. As soon as I heard her car door close, I left the bathroom and asked him who was at the door and he lied and said that it was for his roommate.

I had never seen a roommate the whole time I been coming over here. When do I get to met him? He said, well he works third shift and he stays with his woman a lot. I just stood there listening to him lie to me so skillfully, with a straight face. I was trying to decide whether I should confront him or not; since I knew who the woman was at the door. I knew she did not come to see his roommate. I decided not to confront him because after we made love it was so good. I did not want to have to fight with him. I wanted to have a second round of sex before I went home.

This time I stayed longer than usual. I barely got home before it was time for my dad to get up and get ready for work. The walk home seemed to take forever and my heart ached so bad. I felt like it was broken into a billion pieces. I felt like the biggest fool that ever lived. How could he lie to me as if what he has said was gospel? He seemed to do it with ease. It was as if he was a pro at lying?

Many questions roamed through my mind. Starting with was he using me because he knew I was a virgin? Did he want to be my first love? Why choose me out of all the girls I went to school with? Why did he have to hurt me like this? What did I ever do to deserve this kind of pain? My heart hurted so bad I thought I was going to die from a heart attack. I felt as if God was punishing me because I was having sex with a man that I was not my husband.

I did not ever want to see Mr. Wax again. How could he just lie to me with that straight face? It was as if lying did not faze him one bit. I guess he figured that I was so dumb and stupid. He thought I would believe anything that came out of his lying mouth. For a few days, I avoided talking to him but that did not stop him from calling.

A couple of days later, I broke down and talked to him. He told me how much he missed me and that he needed to see me tonight. He was not taking no for an answer. So I again agreed to see him again after midnight.

What could be so urgent that he had to see me tonight did he want to break up with me? He usually says that he missed me and that he needs to make love to me but not this time. I avoided talking to him for the last few days. I felt this gave him every reason to break up with me. Whatever happens, I could not feel any worse then I was feeling.

I dreaded midnight approaching because part of me did not want to let go of Mr. Wax. Although, I knew he was a lair. I walked slowly to his house and when I got there, he let me in before I could knock on the door. He started kissing me. He held me in his arms and said that he had missed me. He asked what was going on with me. He wondered why I had not called him. I told him that I had been working many hours and by the time I get home, I was exhausted. He said that he wanted to make love to me. It did not sound the same way he used to say it. However, I could not resist him so we made love. As usual, it was good.

Chapter Three: Broken Heart

Two weeks has past, I have not seen Mr. Wax. I am horny and weak. I need to have sex and I do not ever remember feeling like this before. I was hoping he would call and say that he needed to make love to me but he did not.

Although I see many guys at work, none of them seem to be my type. However, they were not him either.

When I least expected it, Mr. Wax called me. I had missed him so much. I could not wait to see him and make love to him again. When I got to his house we sat down on the couch. I thought to myself here it comes; he is going to dump me.

I knew he was wondering why I was not calling him anymore. He asked me if I was seeing someone else? I told him no. I told him that I was still working long hours at work and when I get home my mom makes me clean up the house. I made it seem as though I'd been very tired lately.

He then moved closer to me. He started to rub my arm. Then he put his hand on my thigh and begins to put his hand inside of my panties. Then he put his finger inside of my virgina. He had never done that before. It certainly felt good. Then he begins to kiss me on the lips. Off and on he would push me away. Then he would look at me again and start back kissing me.

I could not figure out why he was pushing me away and looking at me. I thought to myself what was he thinking? What was on his mind? He was kissing me like there was no tomorrow. Although, he was behaving strangely I was into it. By now my panties was soaked and wet. I could not wait to get into the bed and make love to him. Since I think, he is going to end the relationship tonight at this point I will just consider this the last time that we will make love. The last time we would ever touch and kiss each other. I really do not feel as close to him as when I first met him. I just wanted to have sex with him for one reason and that is because I am so horny and I need to have some sex.

When the sex was over, and he acted like it is the best sex he ever had. He said that he is never going to let me go because he loved me so much. I just looked at him because I now see him for the liar he is. It was obvious that he said and did things that were best suited for him and it did not matter whose feelings he hurt.

After sex, I was still debating whether I should confront him by telling him I knew the woman who had came by his house. He told me she was looking for his roommate. I had seen Jan going to her car and I knew her because we were in some of the same classes together. We were in his history class the same hour he taught.

When I looked up, he was staring at me. It was as if he was trying to read my mind. He walked me over to the door. Then he started kissing me. Before I knew it we started to get out of our clothes. This time he did not try to take me to his bedroom we just made love on the couch only this time it did not take long. I was glad because in the bedroom he already acted as if he was trying to kill me. There was something different about this time. He was acting as if he was going away. He was never going to see me again. I do not recall him telling me in one night that he loved me so much. Of course, I do not believe him nor do I trust him but the sex is good it is so hard to resist him.

When I got home, I was so tired. All I wanted to do was sleep for the rest of my life. I went to work. It went by fast. I was glad about that because I was still tired from last night.

When I got home, I ate dinner and cleaned the kitchen. He called and he told me how incredible last night was. He said, he had never felt that way as long as he had been alive and it was the best sex he ever had. I was saying to myself yeah right. I know you are one of the biggest liars that ever lived.

Today is Saturday, I have to work eight hours today, and I am only use to working only five hours a day, so I know this is going to be a long day for me. I went on a lunch break about Noon and I just walked around because I was not hungry. I thought I seen Mr. Wax he was walking fast, as if he did not want me to catch up with him I did not catch up with him. By the time I got to the door where he went out the only thing I could see was the back of his car I looked at the license plates and it was him because his license plates said, "smooth1."

He cannot lie, his way out of this one. I wanted to know why he did not stop to talk to me. What's up with that? When I got home from work I called him to see what was up with him. Also, I wanted to know why he ignored me or acted as if he did not see me. When I know he heard me call his name.

His roommate answered the phone and said, he was not at home. After I hung up the phone, I wondered why I did not ask him when he expected Mr. Wax to be home. I must be losing my mind how would he know when to expect him when he is never at the house.

Two days went by and I haven't heard from him. I am getting worried about him, so I called him again and the roommate answered the phone. Again he said with an angry voice that Mr. Wax doesn't live here anymore. He should have told you that he had gotten married on Saturday. I was silent for a moment. Then I thought that I had heard him wrong. So I asked him to repeat what he had just said to me. He said it again; Mr. Wax had gotten married on Saturday. The roommate said he was sorry and he did not mean to hurt my feelings but you needed to know. He goes on to say that he's sorry about it and the coward son of a b---- should have told you himself. I do not know when he is coming back. He moved all of his things out of here the Thursday before he got married.

On the Friday before he got married we spent the night together. He should have told me then he was getting married. I knew something was wrong because he behaved as if he was never going to see me again.

He never mentioned that he was even seeing someone. That b------d. How could he be engaged to someone and not tell me? He could have told me the truth but I guess he knew he would not be my first love. I was devastated to say the least. I never thought he would hurt me this bad. Why am I so surprise when I seen Jan leaving his house that day? If I was over to his house and he was sleeping with me he had to be sleeping with her too. No telling who else from our school.

I was so angry that I could not see straight. I wanted to crawl up under a rock and die. I just wondered, why he would treat me so bad as if I did not have any feelings at all. I felt like he had treated me like a piece of garbage. I never did anything to hurt anyone in my life and especially him. Oh, Lord what is the matter with me why is this crazy man treating me like this?

I was so depressed and I did not want to live. I thought about what I can do to kill myself. At the same time, I did not wanted to die because I knew if I took my own life, I would go to hell. Hell was not a place I wanted to go. I wondered if that was true or if that is just what Christian, people wanted you to believe. Since I was brought up in the church, I guess I would have to believe that killing yourself is a sin. So I will just have to cope with this situation the best way I can. I wished I had someone to talk to. My best friend went away to college. I feel like a fool. I do not know if I could tell her what he had done to me anyways. Although my younger brother and I are really close. I could not tell him. Because he would tell my other brothers and they would do something to him.

The next day I could hardly get out of the bed. I really did not want to get up but life goes on. I have no choice but to get up. I wondered how will I make it through this day and every other day.

I still have not heard from Mr. Wax and it is Tuesday and I am still mad at him but I still feel that he should be a man about it and tell me himself. But he had gotten married but he did not call me. I am getting worse and worse everyday. I hate to get out of bed. But if I do not get up out of the bed, my family would know that something is wrong with me.

If my brothers' find out what that low life son of b---- did to me they would kill him. My heart still ached and still felt like he had broken it into a billion of pieces. I still had to go on and pretend as if everything was all right. I am tried of pretending as if everything is all right because I am dying on the inside. I do not know where to turn to get some help. Everyday, I want to die and I felt like I was losing my mind.

This week has gone by so slow, it seems as if the time was standing still and I know that is impossible.

Today is Saturday it has been a whole week since Mr. Wax had gotten married. I still have not heard from him but I suppose he is still on his honeymoon. That did not stop me from thinking that he could have found the time to call me, when he was not with her. I begin to wonder if I would ever see him again. I felt crazy for wanting to see him again? I still long to see him and I wanted to feel him make love to me. I was angry with him and I still wanted an explanation as to why he never told me. He was engage to be married. Why would he tell me that he was getting married? He knew I was a virgin. I felt that was all he wanted. What man would turn down the opportunity to have sex with a virgin? I was quiet and shy. He took advantage of my innocence because he knew that I did not know any better. I hate him. However, I still wanted to make love to him, even though he is married. I do not know what is wrong with me or why I still want him in my life, but I do.

The next morning my mom woke me up, so I could get ready for church. I did not want to go to church.

I felt like the Lord had let me down. I did not know how he could let me be in so much pain. Mom came back to my room again because I did not get out of the bed the first time. Now she was rushing me to get dress. Usually, I asked to work on Sundays just so I would not have to go to church but I have not been myself lately.

The pastor preached a good message and it seemed like he had prepared it just for me. I asked God to take away the bad thoughts and to heal my broken heart, so I could get on with my life.

We are now at home. I am helping my mom cook dinner and setting the table. Afterwards, I cleaned up the kitchen. While I was cleaning up the phone rang about three different times. Every time someone answered the phone the person on the other end would hang up. I do not know why but I thought it was Mr. Wax. Why would I want it to be him and he has not called for me in a week and one day. I thought to myself, why would he call now?

I went to the family room to relax before I went to bed. I was sitting in a chair reading a book, when the phone rung. I jumped up as fast I could to be the first one to answer it. I picked it up on the first ring. I said hello and the voice on the other end said hello Danielle I have missed you so much, I need to see you. He begins to apologize to me for not being the person to tell me that he had gotten married. He said that his roommate had no right to tell me. It was none of his business. He said that he did not want to talk on the phone, he wanted to talk to me in person; so I agreed to meet him after midnight.

I sneaked out of the house and when I got to the corner, he was waiting for me in a brand new car with the same license plates smooth1. He took me to an apartment. It was small. It had only one bedroom. When he went to the bathroom, I began to snoop and look around the place to see if I could find a picture of him and his wife. I was curious to see what she looked like. I looked all around and I did not see any signs of a woman living in this apartment. There were no pictures of anyone in sight or out of sight. I did not see him or hear him come back into the room.

I do not know how long he was watching me look around the room. At first, he acted as if he did not know what I was doing but he had a silly grin on his face. Then he said that his wife had left town for the weekend. He then asked me to have a seat and he sat next to me and he begin to tell me that he was sorry and that he never meant to hurt me but he did not know an easy way to tell me that he was engaged to someone. He said after the first time we made love he knew he was in love with me. He knew that I was in love with him. He knew he was my first.

He said that he did not want it to be a bad experience for me and he did not want me to hate all men because of him. I asked him why he did not tell me the first day?

I told him that I should have had the choice to decide whether I wanted to continue seeing him or not. I know you know that I would have seen you until you had gotten married.

He told me that he was in love with me. He could not tell his wife because her father had spent too much money on the wedding. He would kill him if he had called off the wedding at the last minute. He still was proclaiming to be in love with me. He kept making excuses and I was getting tired of hearing them. I told him to stop apologizing to me.

He held me in his arms and said that he will always love me. Then he kissed me and he held me so tight, I could not think straight. I forgot that I was even mad at him I just wanted him to keep holding me and kissing me. We ended up in the bed once again making love. It felt like the earth was moving again it was yet the best sex we had so far. When he was making love to me, he acted as if it was the last time that we would see each other. It was obvious that he was doing all he could to please me and he had never done all these things to me before. I was enjoying every moment because I knew he was saying good-bye to me even if he hadn't said it in words. I was hoping that I was satisfying him like no one ever had including his wife.

I was making sure that he would never forget me and that he would remember that, he was indeed my first love. He held me like the world was ending and I just wanted to enjoy the moment.

In the car on the way home, we did not say too much at first we just listened to the radio and the Isley Brothers was singing Atlantis and he said he was dedicating that song to me because he will always come back to me, even if I decide to get married one day.

I was angry, why he would even think that if I got married I would cheat on my husband. I was not him and I plan on being faithful to my husband. Then he drop the bomb on me that his wife was in Texas looking for them an apartment and that he was leaving the next day.

He said no matter how far away he lived; he would never forget me or stop loving me. He said that we would always love each other. How can this fool tell me that I would always love him?

The longer I sat there the angrier I got. How could I love someone who treats me like crap. Yes, I enjoyed having sex with him but I have not forgiven him for the way he had treated me and besides I was very horny and needed the sex because I have not replaced him yet.

After I got home, I promised myself that I would never sneak out of the house again. I was mad with myself for going to bed with him one more time. I was angry because I did not confront him about Jan my classmate.

I wish I had known her better and had her phone number. I would call her and tell her about Mr. Wax getting married or maybe he have told her already. I wondered if she would want to get even with him or would, she acts like a stupid b---- or if she would want to take her frustrations out on me. I guess that would be crazy to tell her because it was not my place to tell her anyway.

There is no telling how many girls from my school he was sleeping with. Is he a pervert? Did he like sleeping with young girls? I wondered how old is his wife. Was she beautiful, with a nice shape or was she ugly?

He probably was sleeping with the teachers too. The more I thought about it the madder I got. Why did I let him kiss me before I got out of his car? Did he really think that I would forgive him just as if nothing had ever happen? When I got to the house, I was so upset that I don't even remember going into the house and getting into the bed. I was glad that I didn't make any noise because I was so upset and I wasn't in a right frame of mind.

Chapter Four: Deception

I had only four hours of sleep and it was time to get up and go to work. I had a good day at work and time went by quick. When I got home from work, I cleaned up and went to bed. I tossed and turned, I kept thinking about how Mr. Wax dumped me. How he used me I was so angry. I got dressed for work. I kept wondering why I was not a strong person or why did I keep letting him seduce me over and over.

I should have known that he was going to break my heart and make it ache. Why was I so stupid? Why did I have low self-esteem? Why didn't my parents warn me about guys like him? Why didn't they tell me that guys only wanted to have sex and that they really love virgins?

The only things my parents taught me about were the bible and anything to do with church. They acted as if life did not exist outside of church.

What was wrong with me? Was I a cursed Child?

Days and months went by, I was beginning to forget about Mr. Wax. I was feeling better about myself. I decided never to be a man's fool again.

Months had passed and unexpected Mr. Wax called me but I did not talk to him. I told him that I was busy. I could not talk to him right now.

He kept calling me for the next few days but I still did not talk to him. I finally got tired of him calling, so I talked to him. He begin to tell me how much he missed me. He wished he was here, so he could make love to me. I was glad he was far away from me.

I told him that I was finally getting over him. I want him to stop calling me. I told him that I had a boyfriend now. That I had moved on. I told him there was no need for him to call me anymore.

He told me that he loves me. He will never stop loving me and he hoped I was very happy. Then he said good-bye.

I wished it was true but I did not have a boyfriend. I missed not having a man in my life because I was so horny. I do not have a man to sleep with. All I do now is take cold showers and baths. They were not curving my appetite for sex.

I missed the tingling hot sensation between my thighs. I missed my heart skipping a beat or two. I miss a man holding me in his strong arms.

Hell, he could just hold me. Not make love to me. I would be halfway satisfied. Please Lord; do not let some man tell me that he loves me and really do not. I might go postal on the next man who lies to me.

At work, I see at least twenty guys a day. I know I can get anyone of them that I want. I am not ready for a relationship right now. I am lonely as hell and dying to have sex. I am going to wait for the right man to come along.

I miss having sex, just about every man I see looks good to me. I wonder if he is the one that I am going to give myself to. Some days I just want to hook up with a man just for the sex. Then go about my own business. I do not care that I am considered to be a good Christian girl.

The way I see it, is that a Christian girl needs sex too. The only thing I think about these days is sex. I dream about it. I fantasize about sex every chance I get.

I do not care sometimes whether I have sex with a boyfriend or not. I do not care if he is short, tall, big, or skinny I just want some.

I am having dreams and thoughts of sex lately. I must be crazy. I am so horny that I fantasize about being a call girl. I wonder if I am. I had not felt this good in a long time.

What is wrong with me for having these dreams? In order to have these desires and urges, I am addicted to sex. Right now, I wish I could have sex with about three guys at one time. I do not even think that they could satisfy my horny behind right now.

I wonder how many guys it would take to satisfy me. Am I turning into a hoe or is it just a wild fantasy? When I go to bed at night all I dream about is sex. On my lunch break and other breaks, all I think about is sex.

One day, I was at work minding my own business putting merchandise on the racks when a guy came over to me and brushed up against me. He was harder than a brick. As he walked away, he asked me if it was good for me; as it was to him? I said yes.

Then he did it again. It made me so hot and horny. I could not control myself I was too hot to turn off.

I do not know what came over me but we went to the stock room, took off our clothes, and had sex. It happened so quick, I could not believe that I had just had sex with a stranger, I had never seen before, I did not even know his name, and he did not know my name. All I knew is that he had a big juicy penis and he knew how to screw in a few minutes, it was great.

It was exciting and it gave me a rush because no one seen us or busted us in the act. My adrenalin was running high. I was feeling great doing something so crazy. We did not use any protections? How stupid was that? What if he had aids and given it to me? A couple of months back, I would have never done anything so stupid. What is the matter with me? I went back to work like nothing had happened but I was feeling great. I was not horny for now.

The rest of the day flew by. I went home and did the same things I did everyday then I went straight to bed. I woke up the next morning with no problems, except I was soaked and wet but I felt satisfied. I was happy till I got to work. The day was going by slow. So far not very many people came into the store today. Especially not one man came into the store at all. They must know that I am still horny. That is all I think about, day and night; sex, sex, and more sex. I cannot seem to get enough of it. At this point any man would do. I just want to have sex. I do not want a commitment or strings attached. I just want to have sex. I just want to have fun.

The store is about to close in thirty minutes and here comes a lady and her boyfriend. One of the other sales person helped them out. I was glad because I was trying to get things cleaned up so we could leave work on time.

The guy came over to me. He was pretending, to ask me questions about the shirts I was folding. He was really flirting with me. I must admit I was flirting back with him. Until his jealous girlfriend came over to us. She literally dragged him out of the store. I had seen her looking at us. I was just hoping that she would step to me. I would have lost my job today and I would not have cared.

She did the right thing to check her man before she left the store. I feel like you should always check your partner and not the other person.

When I got off work, my mom had to wait on me. It took us a little longer to clean up tonight. She complained about how the house was dirty and that the kitchen was a mess, with the dirty pots and pans still on the stove empty with food caked on them.

I am thinking to myself, what the hell was everyone else doing, while I am at work. Why can't they clean up after themselves? I have not been home to mess anything up. I am tired. I worked eight hours today. All I want to do is go to bed. I finished cleaning up around the house. Now I cannot wait to get into my bed.

As soon as my head hit the pillows. I was out like a light and I dreamed about being a call girl again.

This time I am at an expensive restaurant with a millionaire. He had the owner of the restaurant to close the place, so we could dine alone. We danced and ate a lovely dinner.

He took me to a five star hotel; we just talked. He told me all about his wife. He said that he did not want to have kids but she did. He said that she did not pay enough attention to him as it was. He told me what kind of sex he wanted. I took the money first and then lock it up in the safe. Then I hid the key. I made sure he had protection. The sex was great. He gave me a hundred dollar tip and said that he would see me next week.

Chapter Five: Fantasy Shopping

Time for work and my mom is on the phone. She does not like to be interrupted but I had twenty minutes to get to work on time. I do not like to be late for work. I wished I had my own car. I would not have to depend on my mom to get me to work. I know that I would never be late for work. I can forget about a car because I do not make enough money to make a car payment. It is another slow day at work and I am bored.

I am hoping that my manager would ask me to go home early today. She asked the other girls if they wanted to go home early but they said no. She asked me and I said yes.

After I clocked out, I begin to think why in the world, would I want to go home early. Home was the last place in the world I wanted to be. Therefore, I did not call my mom to come and get me. Even though I have three hours before she comes to pick me up from work. I know I can find something to do till she come to pick me up. The first place I went was to a jewelry store. Now I know I cannot afford a gold chain, diamond, or anything else in here. Nevertheless, that did not stop me from looking around. I saw an emerald ring and I love emeralds. It had some diamonds around it. I asked the sale person if I could try the ring on and it was a perfect fit. I asked the sales woman how much the ring cost and she said four thousand and fifty dollars. I sadly gave her the ring back. I wished I had some kind of credit card, because I really wanted that ring. It was a perfect fit and it did not need to be sized. The next place on my agenda was Victoria Secrets. I wanted to see what looked good on me; instead of just fantasizing about it. I wanted to see the real deal on me. There were a lot of lingerie I could afford. I knew I could not take any of it home because my mom still goes threw my closets and drawers. If she seen them she would make me throw them away. I did not want my hard earned money go down the drain.

I was hungry, so I went to get me something to eat. I already knew what I wanted to eat. I ordered a cheeseburger, fries and a small coke. I spotted the perfect table with two chairs and a perfect view. I could see everyone come in and see everyone who leaves.

I was dipping my fries in some ketchup, when I looked up a man was standing over me. He asked if he could sit down with me and of course, I said yes.

He was about six feet five. He did not look bad but he was not fine either. He was wearing a nice navy blue suit with the tie to match. He had on navy blue shoes. He was clean from head to toe. He smelled good, which was a plus.

We sat there at first not saying anything to each other. Then he broke the silence first. He asked me if I was married. I told him no. I asked him if he was married? He said no.

Then I asked him how old was he? He said he was twenty-six. I told him that I was eighteen. I really wanted to lie and say I was twenty-five but I figure why lie.

Then he said that is not bad. I asked him what did he mean by that statement? He said that I was of legal age. If we wanted to date each other it would be okay. He asked me if I wanted to go somewhere quiet? I said yes. I knew I should not go anywhere with a stranger but my instincts told me that he was all right. Therefore, I went with him. On the way to his car, I told him that I had to be back at the mall in two hours because my mom was going to pick me up at that time. He said that was more than enough time to get to know each other.

He asked me was there is a special place that I wanted to go? I said yes. I would like to go to a park that has a beautiful dam and the lights are different colors at night. It was not dark enough to see the lights but that is where I wanted to go. I love to look at the water and hear the sound of the water going over the dam. It was very soothing, just listening to the water. Besides it is a public place in case he tried something crazy; there are other people around to help me. I felt safe in a public place with a man I did not know. It took us ten minutes to get there from the mall.

When we got there, he got out of his car. He opened my door as he had done at the mall to let me into the car. I thought what a perfect gentleman. I was very impressed with him because I never had anyone to open a door for me. My dad did not even open the car door for my mom. I felt that he must be special and the perfect guy for me.

We had the perfect seat at the park. We were directly over the dam. We could see the water going over the edge without us having to stand up and look over the ledge.

The sound of the water was very soothing. It made me

relaxed as I had expected. I decided to get up and look over the ledge to see if the lights were on. I had never been to the park this early in the day.

As I looked on, I was in deep thought. He grabbed me and put his hands around my waist. He said that he would give me a penny for my thoughts.

I said okay and he gave me a penny. I made a wish and threw it in the water. He asked me what I had wished for. Then I laughed. I turned to him and said that I think I must be crazy. I have rode this far with you and I don't even know your name. You don't know my name either.

He said your name is Danielle. How did you know my name? I have not told you my name? I started to get a little nervous. Is this man a stalker? I hope he is not crazy or a psycho killer.

He told me that his name is Jason. He was a doctor at the main hospital in town. Wow, I thought to myself I have just hit the jackpot. The man opens the doors for me, he is a doctor, and he looks good at that. What more could I ask for in a man.

Jason put his hand around my waist and pulled me close to him. As we looked at the water I was thinking that he needed to let me go because I was really getting horny. My nipples were hard and sticking straight out. I could feel a bulge, I tried to determine the size of his penis but I could not. I started to grind up against him and we both were grinding together. People were around us. We did not want to draw any attention to us, so we stopped before we got too far out of hand. I could hear him breathing real heavy and it was turning me on but I didn't want him to think I was a whore on the first time we met. Therefore, I restrained myself and I just enjoyed his hard penis pressed up against me. I thought it was a good time to tell him about my family.

I told him that I was the only girl out of four. I was the baby of the family and my three brothers are very protective of me. He asked if I got special treatment since I was the baby and the only girl? I wish that was the case but it was not. You can say that I am the family slave instead of part of the family.

My brothers think I should clean up after them. I iron their clothes and my mom goes along with it. Even though they are all older than I am. She says that I am a girl and I need to learn how to do these things because one day I am going to get married. My husband will expect me to know how to do everything around the house.

I do not know how she figures that I am going to get married one day. She will not let me date anyone. She won't even let me talk to a guy on the phone. My brothers are very protective of me. They would give any guy the third degree who is interested in me. Of course, I do not have to worry about any guys coming to visit me at my parent's house. They will not allow him to come in. I told him that my oldest brother is fifteen years older than I am. I do not know too much about him but I know that he loves me even though he is married and has two children. My middle brother is ten years older than I am. He just got married. We got along good. My baby brother is just a year older than I am. We are thick as thieves. He is my best friend and when we were little, he would let me play basketball with him and his friends. Even though they did not want me to play with them. I love David; he is the best brother in the world.

Jason said that he was the only child. He wished that he had a sister or brother. He said that he had never met his father. At this point in his life, his father is dead to him. He gives his mother all the credit for all of his accomplishments. I did not want to leave the park. However, I had to get back to the mall before my mom got there.

When we got back the mall he opened the door and let me out. He gave me a kiss and a card with his phone number. He told me to call him, when I got home. He asked me for my cell number. I told him that I didn't have one and he gave me his phone and told me to only use it when he called me. I said okay and went into the mall.

When my mom got there, she was in a good mood. She did not mention anything to me about cleaning up the house. I have never had such a great day like this before. I felt like I was dreaming. For the first time Jason made me forget about Mr. Wax. When I got home, I ate and cleaned up and went to bed. This was the first time in weeks I did not dream of being a call girl. I dreamed about Jason all night long. I dreamed that he was the guy in my dreams that took me to the fancy five star restaurants and hotel. I dreamed that we slow danced and made passionate love all night long. I woke and could not believe that Jason and I did not make love yesterday.

On the way to work, my cell phone rung. I really could not talk because my mom was listening. I told him that I would call him when I get into the mall. My mom asked me where did I get the phone? I told her that a girl from work gave it to me. I just have to make the payments. I was surprised that she did not give me the third degree. I hurried out of the car so I could call Jason. He said that he had Wednesdays off and he wanted to spend the whole day with me. I said okay.

When Tuesday came around, I told my mom that on tomorrow I would have to go into work at seven in the morning. She asked my why I had to go in so early tomorrow? I usually have to be there at ten. I told her that I had to do inventory tomorrow so I had to be there early before the store opens. She dropped me off. She kept on going as usual. I was glad she did not wait to watch me go in because Jason was already there and waiting for me. I walked over to his car. He met me before I could get to the car door and he opened the door for me. When he got in the car, he reached over and kissed me on the lips. I always knew that kissing could lead to other things like sex. I did not want the first with Jason to be in his car. So I pulled back away from him.

We went to his apartment, which is located close to downtown not far from the hospital where he works. When we pulled in front of his building, he opened the door. We went inside and instead of taking the elevator; we walked up two flights of stairs. He said that is how he gets his exercise everyday.

When he opened the door to his apartment, it was just gorgeous. It looked like he had an interior designer to decorate his place. He said he did it all by himself. Everything was neat and in place. I could not help but think that he and my mom would get along just fine as clean as his apartment was. He had the perfect view of the city. The buildings were all different sizes and different shapes. I tell you this is the perfect place to live I thought to myself.

I sat in his lap and we begin to kiss. He must be the best kisser in the world because I really enjoy his soft big lips on my lips. Today nothing is going to stop us from making love. He picked me up, carried me to his bed, and laid me down softly. He gently started to kiss me on my lips and on my neck, and he gave me a hickey. The next thing I knew we were taking each other's clothes off and now it was time for what I had been waiting for.

We made love for a whole fifteen minutes. I could not believe he was finished. I just thought he was taking a break. I am glad that was over. He was not a better lover than Mr. Wax; although his penis was bigger. Hell, he was not as good as the guy I had sex with in the stock room at work. Before he could ask me if the sex was good, his pager went off. He had to go to work. What perfect timing because I did not want to lie to him. I guess I could not tell him the truth either.

He called the hospital and they needed him right away. We took a shower together. Then he dropped me off at the mall. I had to keep myself busy for two hours before my mom would come and get me. I was a pro at it now. I could call my mom and told her that I have gotten off work early but I did not want to be at home.

I got hungry so I went to get me something to eat. I went to a furniture store. I pretended that I was buying furniture for my new apartment. It was almost time for my mom to pick me up. I had to hurry to the other side of the mall because my mom did not like to be waiting for me.

The next day Jason called to say that he enjoyed yesterday. He cannot wait to see me again. I wish I could say the same about him. The only reason I wanted to be with him is so I would not have to be at home. Oh, he is a great kisser. He asked if I could see him tomorrow and I said yes.

I woke up the next morning, not really looking forward to seeing him. We sat on the bed watching television for a while then we started to kiss. I just loved the way he kissed. Only if he could make love the way he kissed. I would never want to leave him. We kissed for a little while longer. He got up and went to his suit coat pocket, and he put it behind his back and walked over to me. I was trying to see how big the box was but I could not see the box.

He gave me the box. I quickly opened it up, because I was anxious to see what was inside it. After I saw the emerald ring, I went into shock. This man obliviously has good taste or he can read my mind. He took the ring out of the box and put it on my finger. I was so excited; I asked him how he knew that I like emeralds?

He said that the day we met he seen me in the jewelry store. He saw how much I adored the ring. After I left he asked the sales person to show him the ring that I was admiring. Once again, he freaked me out. After looking at the ring the feelings soon went away.

I jumped up off of the bed, kissed, and hugged him. He kissed me back he said that he was glad that he could make me happy. We kissed and we fell on to the bed. We made love. I got caught up in the moment. I had forgotten about the last time we had sex and how bad it was. I was so horny that any sex was better than no sex. Also, I was just so happy to get that beautiful emerald ring. Sleeping with him would be the least I can do to show him my gratitude.

Chapter Six: A Big Decision

When we were finished making love, he asked me to move in with him. I looked at him like he was crazy or something. I was definitely lost for words. I did not expect him to ask me something like that. I told him that we have not known each other long enough for me to move in with him. He said two months is long enough to know whether you like a person or not.

He said that he knew the moment he saw me that we were going to be together. We were going to get married and have some children. He was freaking me out again. I told him that my parents would be very angry and they will try to stop me from leaving their house.

Anyway, I would not know how to tell them that I am moving in with you. In the meantime, I could hardly get over thinking about the bad sex either.

Jason said would you like me to go with you? We can tell them together that you are moving in with me.

No, I said. I think it would be best if I just told them alone. If you are there that will just make them even angrier. Who knows my brothers will probably try to hurt you.

He then asked, does that mean that you are trying to avoid moving in with me?

No, I said. I want to live with you. I just think we need to get to know each other better.

He said that he knew everything about me that he needed to

know. He kind of reminded me of Mr. Wax and how persuasive he could be.

Once again, against my better judgment, I agreed to move in with him, if he let me tell my parents; when I was ready to tell them. He backed off and said okay.

He took me home and this time he dropped me off directly in front of my house. My mom was in the kitchen window. When I got inside, she asked me who dropped me off. I lied to her and said a girl that I worked with brought me home. She did not fuss at me, so I knew she did not see who drove the car.

All I could think about is how I will tell my parents that I wanted to move out of their house and be my own woman. I knew that they were not going to be happy with my decision. I am sure they still think that I am a virgin. I guess it is going to rock their world when I tell them that I am moving out.

In a way, I could not wait to see their faces. What could they do? They cannot stop me from leaving because I am eighteen years old. I called Jason and he asked me if my parents had gotten mad at me because he dropped me off at home? I told him no. They did not see who was driving the car.

I could tell by his voice that he was mad. He said that he was a grown man and he was tired of sneaking around to be with me. I should be able to date without supervision of my parents. He said that I am a woman now and I should be making decisions like an adult. While he was talking the bad sex memory kept roaming through my mind.

The tone he took with me was, if I was a child. My parents had never spoken to me like that. He was right I needed to start standing up for myself. I needed to start with making decisions for myself. I decided that at the end of the week, I would tell my parents that I would be moving out. I could not wait to move away from my parents. I wanted to see what it was like on the outside world. The only thing I was allowed to do was to go to church and to work. Everything else was off limits to me. I wanted to learn how to skate, bowl, play cards and I wanted to go to a nightclub and maybe go to a concert or two. It will be great to be on my own.

I was at work when Jason called me. I was surprised because I have not heard from him in two days. I asked him if he was still mad at me. He said that he was not mad at me. He said he had to pull a double shift. He said that he was mad at the way my parents had raised me. He wanted to see me, so I told him to pick me up at the mall. He said here we go again. I told him if he did not want to see me, he did not have to come and get me at all.

He picked me up at the mall anyways. We went back to his place. We really did not do any kissing or talking for that matter. We did make love. He took me back home. I was surprised that he did not force the issue of me telling my parents that I was moving out. When I got home I decided that I would tell my parents tomorrow. He was happy to hear that I had finally set a date to tell them.

I asked him if he was going to be waiting outside of my parent's house while I tell them. He asked what time did I want him to be there and I said about five o'clock p.m. He said okay that he would be there. I was glad that I did not have to work for the next three day. I was walking around the house trying to figure out the best way to tell my parents that I am moving out today.

As I cleaned up my bedroom, I tried to practice saying the words in my head over and over. Dad came home from work, so I knew I had only an hour before Jason would get here. We were about to sit down for dinner and I told my parents, I had something to tell them after dinner.

My mom said that I had better not be pregnant. I said you are not going to like what you are about to hear. Do not worry mom. I am not pregnant. Mom said you do not have to wait until after dinner you can tell us now. The doorbell rung and my youngest brother David said Danielle it is for you. Jason what are you doing here it is not four thirty yet. You said that you were going to wait in the car for me. I was but I thought you would need my support to help you tell your parents. Well you are here now, so I guess I can introduce you to my family. He followed me to the dining room; I introduce everybody to each other.

Then Jason told my family that we were in love and I was moving in with him. I promise you that I will take good care of Danielle. My mom jumped in front of me and told me that I was not going anywhere but to my bedroom. I told her that I was old enough to make my own decision and I am leaving.

My mom asked my dad to do something to stop me from leaving. My dad turned to me and said that he loved me. He will always love me. Then he gave me a hug. He said I wish you would stay here with your mom and me but I cannot make you stay against your will.

I cannot give you my blessings because I do not know anything about Jason. I will be praying for you. My mom said is that all you are going to do and he said yes. I got my clothes and we left.

On the way to Jason's apartment, I did not say a word I was feeling sad. The way my mom looked and behaved it seemed as if she was having a heart attack. I was her only girl how did I expect her to act?

I was surprised at how well my dad handled me leaving. I knew he always wanted the best for me, but I did not really know exactly how much he loved me. The things he said made me feel a little better.

I do not know how my mom feels about me. She never gave me a hug or told me that I did a good job at anything. We took my things into the apartment, I was glad that I did not have many clothes because we walked up the two flights of stairs; instead of taking the elevator. I thought that was stupid.

I believe in getting exercise. I thought to myself what was the point, of going up the stairs? There was an elevator in the building that works. I knew I would never get use to this.

He showed me were to put my clothes. He said make yourself comfortable in your new home because you live here now. I felt as if I was dreaming, although my parents have a beautiful home this apartment was like paradise. I did not have to answer to my parents all the time. I bet I will get some peace and quiet now.

When Jason went to work it was very quiet. This is the first time I would be alone. I did not know what I was going to do my first night in the apartment alone. I got me a book and curled up in the bed and the next thing I knew it was morning. Jason was in the shower getting ready to get into the bed. He asked me to get back in the bed with him because he didn't want to sleep alone anymore. I got back into the bed. He asked me how did I like being on my own. I said I would have loved my first night here with him sleeping next to me.

I thought we were going to make love but he was fast asleep. I just laid there and wondered what my mom was doing. Was she still mad at me? Will she ever get over the fact that I am not her little girl anymore? I hope that one day when I have kids; I will let them go when they are old enough to be on their own.

Only after a week of living with Jason, he asked me to quit my job. Like an idiot, I quit my job because he said that it was his job to take good care of me. The only way he could do that is for me to be at home.

Months had gone by and things were going along good until a guy called and asked for Jason. He said that he had heard that Jason had lost a patient today. I told him that he was not here. I asked him for his name. He said that he would just go ahead and page Jason.

This must be the first patient he had lost. I wondered who was that guy on the phone. Was he a doctor Jason worked with? I hope Jason was all right I have not heard from him today. Maybe he is out having drinks with some of the doctors he worked with. They are probably consoling him.

It's midnight and I know he got off work five hours ago. Where is he? I still have not heard from him, so I decided to go to bed. I heard him come in about four o'clock in the morning and he went straight to the bathroom and took a shower. When he got into the bed, he turned his back to me. He had never done that before. I thought we were tighter than that.

I just pretended to be asleep. He tossed and turned the whole time his was asleep. It is nine o'clock in the morning. I cannot sleep; I am not use to being in the bed at this time of the day. Therefore, I ease on out of the bed.

It is about noon and he is sleeping well. I just looked in on him. I did not wake him because I assumed that he did not have to work today. He finally woke up and he said that he was going back to bed. He wanted me to join him so I did. He held me in his arms. He told me what had happened at work. He talked about a patient he had operated on. The patient died two hours later.

He said that he felt like a failure and that losing a patient was devastating to him. I tried my best to comfort him and convince him that he was not a failure. I told him that I loved him very much.

I told him that I would do anything to cheer him up and that got his attention. That seemed to perk him right up. It got his mind off work. He instantly had a devilish grin on his face. He told me that he wanted to have sex and he wanted me to take control and be in charge.

Okay, I can do this I said to myself but have he lost his mind. He knows how shy I am. I know he must be testing me. I had to think of something right quick. I remember on one of the X-Rated video that we watch, he was all into one of the scenes. I thought reliving that scene would be the perfect treat for him.

I stood up in the bed directly over him. I begin to dance. I looked down at him and it was turning him on. I lowered my body down close to his but I did not make contact with his body. Then I put my tongue in his ear and then I licked his neck. I lick his nipples then I licked his navel. I went down to his penis. I heard him make noises and sounds I never heard him make. I must be doing a good job. Even if this is the first time that I have went down on anyone.

He was begging me not to stop because it was feeling so good. I had never made him feel that good. Next thing I knew he was saying that he was about to come, so I stopped.

He asked me what I was doing, so I pushed him back on the bed then I got on top of him. I rode him as if I was a cowgirl at a rodeo. I enjoyed being on top. I enjoyed being in control. I can get use to this.

This was the first time we had good sex. I really enjoyed it. After we got finished, we both were fast asleep. He slept like a baby. He hadn't gotten that much sleep in a while. The next morning he went to work. He seemed to be a little depressed but I suppose after losing a patient, he would not feel like going to work. He should expect to lose a patient every once in awhile in his line of work.

I know it is not going to be pleasant or easy to handle. As the weeks went by he was getting better. He was not thinking about the patient that he had lost anymore. He seemed to be in good spirits.

One night he came home from work, I had fell asleep and left the radio on. He got very mad at me, and he had a fit. I knew something had to be bothering him because leaving a radio on all night was not a big deal. I had never seen him behave like this before.

When he woke up, I told him that he was talking in his sleep again. He asked me what he was saying; I told him that I could not make out the words. I just knew he was talking in his sleep. He got angry with me and called me a liar. He said if he was talking in his sleep I would remember everything he said; because that is the way women are.

The next thing I knew, he had hit me so hard in my right eye. It hurt me so bad. I thought I was seeing bright stars. I could not think straight or see straight. I must be dreaming because the man I love is a perfect gentleman. I know he would never harm me.

When I came to myself, I was lying in the bed in Jason's arms. I had no knowledge of how I got there. I tried to move but he was holding me so tight that I could not move. He told me that he was so sorry. He said he didn't know what had come over him. He had never hit a woman before in his life.

He promised me that he would never hit me again. He said that he was truly sorry. I am thinking to myself, why I had to be the first woman he hit? I was afraid of him. I just wanted to get out of that bed. He begin to kiss me. It felt like my skin was crawling. I did not want him to touch me anymore. He made love to me. I wanted him to stop but I was afraid to tell him to get off me after what he had done to me earlier.

It felt like he was rapping me. With every other stroke he made, he kept telling me that he was sorry. I certainly did not feel like he loved me. I had never done anything to hurt him. You don't hurt someone you love.

What was wrong with this crazy man? I thought to myself what other secrets is he hiding from me? He continued to say, he was sorry. He sounded like a broken record that needed to be dumped into the garbage. I am tired of hearing I am sorry. I did not know what to do.

He got up and got ready for work I usually got up with him but not today, I decided to stay in bed. Before he left, he kissed me on my eye. He said he was sorry. If he did not have to go to work and make some money, he would stay home to make me feel better.

I was glad he was leaving; I wished he had to work a double shift. I did not want to see his face. I did not want him to touch me.

After he left for work, I heard some noise outside of my door in the hallway. I went to the door and looked out in the hall but no one was out there. As I was, about to close my door the neighbor across the hall came out. She asked me if I had heard some noise in the hall and I said yes.

She invited me to come inside of her apartment. She introduced herself to me. She said that her name is Tonya. I told her that my name was Danielle.

She told me that she was married. She didn't have any kids and that she wasn't ready for any either. She said that she was twenty-two years old. I told her about my family and me.

She said you are not going to tell me about that fine man you live with. When I was talking about my family, I had completely forgotten about Jason. I said yes of course we are not married and I do not want any kids either.

I had forgotten about my black eye until she asked me what had happened to my face. I did not feel like making up a lie so I told her that Jason hit me. I tried to change the subject and tell her that I did not have any friends that I could confide in because my best friend went away to college. I told her that my mom and I did not get along and I have not seen her or my family in a year.

She told me that I could come over and talk to her anytime. She said you know you should leave him before things get worse.

Once a guy hit you, he is going to hit you again. Trust me take it from someone who knows first hand and been there in your shoes. I had a boyfriend who use to beat me whenever he felt like it. One day he shot me in the leg because he did not give me permission to leave the house.

I told her that Jason was not like that. She said yeah after he hit you, he told you repeatedly that he was sorry. He had never hit a woman before, and that he did not know what had came over him.

Then he made love to you and told you that he would never hit you again.

They make love to you because they think that is your weakness. They feel the intimacy will make you forgive them for anything, especially if they put it on you right. Danielle please do not believe him. He is lying to you because he cannot help himself. You can be sure that he will hit you again; when something else makes him mad. I told her that I could not leave him. I kept thinking to myself I had nowhere to go. When I left home, my mom said that I could not come back there to live. Tonya told me, she would take me to the shelter for battered women. That is where she went and got her life back on track. I told her that if he hit me again, I would take her up on her offer.

I went back to my apartment and watched the television, until I got sleepy. It seemed like Jason was never at home anymore. Maybe he was really sorry and ashamed for hitting me.

It was getting close for the hospital charity ball. I was looking forward to having a good time. Jason took me shopping for a dress, purse, and some shoes. I saw a beautiful long light blue dress with a split up the side. It was cut low in the front and the back neckline was in a V-Shape.

Jason did not like the dress; he said that it was not classy enough. He picked me out a long plain black dress with the accessories to match. I did not like the dress but he reminded me that he was paying for it.

What has happened to him? This is not the man I met at the

mall. He is not the person I fell in love with. He is too controlling. Where is the man I met a year ago?

This is the day of the ball and I must admit that Jason looked good in his black tuxedo and I do not remember ever seeing him looking that good. I put on my dress and it did not look bad. In fact, the dress looked good on me. I had gotten my hair done and my nails done for the first time in my life. Jason kept staring at me saying how beautiful and gorgeous I looked.

He said that he hated to take me out and have to share me with his co-workers. Before we left, he gave me a beautiful diamond necklace and matching earrings. They were so beautiful they went really well with my dress.

I had fun at the ball. I met many interesting people. I had fun dancing. We had practiced for a month. I felt like Cinderella. I had never felt this beautiful before. When we got home, the two of us were tired, so we just went straight to bed. We did not talk or make love we just went to sleep.

The next day, when he went to work the phone kept ringing. Every time I picked up the phone, no one would say anything. But I could hear the person breathing. I looked at the caller ID but it said private number. The phone rung and I was about to cuss the person out when Jason said hi. He said that he would not be home tonight because he had to work a double shift.

Okay I said and hung up the phone. I went over to Tonya's place and played bid whiz with her and her husband. It was fun I had never played cards before. In fact I enjoyed bid whiz. My parents said it was a sin to play cards. I never knew why they believed that.

All I know is that I had fun playing cards today. They said I caught onto bid whiz quick. The next time they would show me how to play another game. They told me anytime I get bored and did not have anything to do, just come on over.

I was cleaning the apartment. I begin to think about how much I missed my family especially my youngest brother David. We use to be close. I have not seen my mom or dad in a year. I have not talked to them either. I decided to call my parents house. My youngest brother picked up the phone on the first ring. I said hello. He said hello back. He said that he and my other brothers would still go to the store in the mall where I use to work, hoping to see me but I would not be there.

I could not tell him that Jason made me quit my job. I asked him how were mom and dad doing? He said that they were doing well and he thinks they miss me but they just were too stubborn to admit it to anyone.

I heard Jason put his keys in the door. I tried to hurry up and get off the phone. I said good-bye and tell everyone that I love them. He said that he loved me and missed me a whole lot and he could not wait to see me.

Jason asked me who was I talking to and telling them that I loved them. I told him that I was talking to my youngest brother. He screamed at me why are you talking to your family, they treated you like yesterday's garbage. I take care of you. Don't you forget that.

It's My Life   70

You do not need them you have me.

I told him that I miss my family and I did not say that I wanted to move back home with my parents. He said I know that you are not getting smart with me. I said no. He walked toward me and he grabbed me by my neck. He begin to choke me. I was trying to push him off me but I could not breathe. He let go of me and I do not know what made him let go of my neck but I was glad. For a minute I thought I was going to die. He pushed me away and then he walked towards the door.

Before I could catch my breathe good, he was walking towards me again. He asked me if I had anything to say to him and I didn't say anything. He just punched me so hard that I fell on the floor. As he came toward me I started to cry and scream from the top of my lungs leave me alone. Then he started kicking me everywhere. I could feel blood coming out of my mouth. It seemed like the room had turned black. I could not see anything. I could hear him crying and saying that he was sorry and he love me more than life it self. He left the apartment, I did not know where he was going, and I did not care either.

He scared me to death. I just knew he was going to kill me tonight. I kept thinking to myself. Why did he think my family was a threat to him? This man is crazy. I have to get out of here but I could not move. I heard someone knocking on the door, I asked who it was, and it was Tonya. I told her that I could not move to go and get the manager to let her into my apartment. She went to get the manager and her husband.

They came into the apartment. I still could not see anything. Tonya and her husband gathered my clothes and carried me to the car. They asked what hospital they should take me. I freaked out and said that he worked at the hospital and I did not trust going to any hospital, so they took me to the shelter for battered women.

When I got to the shelter, a woman doctor looked at me. She took glass out of my leg and told me that I was lucky because the glass just missed one of my main arteries. She checked both of my eyes they were both completely close shut. She said my eyes would be all right in a couple of weeks. She looked and my neck where he had left a mark.

She asked me if I wanted her to call the police, so I could prosecute the man that did this to me. I said no. She asked me why not? I said because he is a doctor. I do not what to ruin his career. He has been under a lot of stress lately. She said that is not an excuse for anyone to hit another person.

We all have some type of stress; we have to deal with everyday. If he is a doctor, he should know better because it is his job to save lives and not to take a life. She said that it was her job to report the crime. She said that I did not have to give the police his name but I did have to see the police. I said okay. When the cops got there they took pictures of my neck, legs, back, and my eyes. They asked me if I was sure that I did not want to press charges against the animal that did this to me. I said no.

They told me if I changed my mind that my file would be downtown at the police station. The doctor came back into my room and told me to take it easy for a couple of weeks. She said that I had a concussion. I needed to stay in the bed for a couple of days and stay off my feet.

I thanked Tonya and her husband for helping me and for saving my life. They told me to get some rest and they would come and see me tomorrow. We said our good byes and I went to sleep. I did not think about Jason. I guess I was in too much pain to think about him.

The medication the doctor gave me was kicking in. I woke up the next day and I still could not see out of either or my eyes at all. I am still in a state of shock. It feels like I am still dreaming. Why did he go postal on me? I do not ever want to see him again. Why did I get involved with him anyway? It is not as if he satisfied me sexually anyways. How can a man with a big penis not know how to use it? Something is seriously wrong with that crazy man. Something must be wrong with me for getting involved with him, when my gut instinct was telling me to leave him alone.

I guess you should always listen to your inner self.

Chapter Seven: Time to Get on my Feet

A month had pass, I was still living in the shelter. All I did was go to group meetings and listened to the other women talk about what had happened to them, and a few times, I would talk about what happened to me.

One day Tonya and her husband came to visit me and they took me to one of their friend's house. We played cards until eight thirty. I had to be back at the shelter at nine O'clock p.m.

Tonya's husband told me that a guy at the accountant firm where he worked needed a secretary. He told him that I was the perfect person for the job. He had made an appointment for Monday at nine in the morning. I told him that I would be there early. I needed some money because I was tired of staying at the shelter. I wanted to get my own place. I am ready to take control of my life and live it my way.

I got to the office fifteen minutes early. The man was not there yet. I did not mind because I knew I was early for my appointment. I always like to be early. I rather be early than late and I really needed a job.

When he came in he walked pass me and went into his office. Five minutes later his secretary told me that I could go in his office now.

He asked me if I could type. I told him yes, so the secretary took me to a room and gave me a typing test. I typed seventy-five words in a minute with two errors. He asked me if I knew how to use a computer. I replied yes. He said that he needed me to start to work right away.

I was so happy I could have done a happy dance but I was in public, so I kept my happiness inside of me. He then introduced me to Judy the secretary who told me to go into his office. He told me that Judy was going to show me the ropes and if I had any questions, she would help me out. Judy showed me around the office and introduced me to the other co-workers. She gave me the 411 on all of them.

I liked her because she was a down to earth person. She said whatever was on her mind. I thought that was good. She would tell me where I stood and if I was doing everything right or if I was doing something wrong. I knew we were going to get along just fine.

The only problem is that I have always been a loner. I did not like to associate with many people. For lunch, I would spend it alone. I needed quiet time for myself. Besides, I figured if I spend lunch, alone I would not have to be in the middle of some type of mess or gossip.

Once a week, I would go out with the girls after work. Three months later and I was still working at the accountant firm. I had saved enough money to get an apartment. I looked for weeks trying to find the perfect place with the salary I was making. I was not going to live in a dump. Finally, I came across the perfect one bedroom apartment, it was just two blocks away from where I worked, and I could walk.

I went to the furniture store in the mall. I purchased bedroom furniture and a dining room set. It felt great to be on my own and paying my own rent. The best part is that I did not have anyone telling me what to do or how to do it. Thank God, I am truly a free woman with no man in my life controlling me and telling me what to do. I even purchased a gun for protection. I decided to go to the shooting range to learn how to properly use it. No one will ever hurt me again. Thanks to Jason, I do not have an urge or desire for sex anymore and I do not know if that is a good thing or not.

All I know is that I am feeling great about myself and I do not need a man in my life right now. All I want to do now is to better my life. I wanted to have something meaningful. I wanted to show myself that I can achieve anything I put my mind to.

My boss told me that since I have worked more than ninety days at the company they will pay me to go to college. However, I would have to pay for my own books. I went to the community college and registered for some accounting classes. I figure it would help me get a promotion and help me improve my skills at the office.

Two years has passed. I cannot believe that I am graduating with my associate degree in accounting. I called my brothers and told them the good news. I was graduating on Saturday. I was surprised to see all three of them sitting close to the front. They cheered loudly for me as I walked across the stage and received my degree. After the ceremony, they took me out to dinner and we talked about mom and dad. I invited them to come over to see my apartment.

They said that I had good taste in furniture and they were not surprised at all, since our mom had great taste. I offered them something to drink. We talked about the good ole days. I told them how much I had missed them, mom, and dad too.

Even though I always sent my parents cards on their birthdays, Easter and Christmas, it just was not the same as seeing them. I do not even know if they opened the cards or read them. They never sent me any cards. It did not matter. I just wanted them to know how much I missed them and that I still love them. I hated to see my brothers leave but it was getting late.

I was glad it is Sunday because yesterday seemed to tire me out. I hope to see more of my brothers because I really enjoyed their company. I had told them not to be like strangers since they know where I lived. When I got to work on Monday, Judy insisted that I go to lunch with her. She wanted to celebrate my graduation since I did not spend Friday with the girls.

Before lunch, she said she needed to go to one of the boardroom and get some papers she left in there earlier. We went into the boardroom and everyone shouted. For she is a jolly good fellow!

I was truly surprised they had pizza, cake, ice cream and

soda. I could not believe that they cared that much about me. My boss said that I was the first person in the office to take advantage of the education program.

A month later, I got a promotion as a supervisor. I love my job and the raise is great. I have my own office now. Judy had not changed since I was her boss now. We were still cool but the other women had attitudes. They were player hating me. I made enough money now, I could afford a car. I would not have to catch the bus when it rained or when it was just too cold to walk to work.

I called Tonya and asked her if they could go with me to buy a car. I did not want the sales person to take advantage of me since I did not know anything about cars. They met me at a car dealership after I got off work.

I bought a purple Sebring convertible with a black top. I looked great in this car. I let the top down and pulled out of the parking lot heading for home. Wow, what a great feeling nothing could top this feeling except when I got my apartment.

Now this is how an independent woman is supposed to feel. This is my life and I will live it the way that I want. I feel great. This must be the greatest high ever. I am enjoying not depending on a man for anything. Anything I needed, I can buy for myself. I am finally in control of my life. I am very proud of myself it took me long enough to get here. I am glad that I had faith in myself.

This is an awesome day for me. I learned today that I could do whatever I put my mind to. I promise myself that I will not be conceded just, because I bought a new car. I was happy that I did not have to depend on anyone to pick me up I could come and go when I get ready.

At work, everyone noticed my car and they told me that they loved my car and that they knew I was happy to have my own wheels. I thanked them for their compliments and went to work.

Christmas is in two weeks. I have not seen my parents in three years, so I plan to give them a surprise visit for Christmas. I am going shopping for them as soon as I get out of work today. I saw a fur coat in one of the store windows. I went in to look at the coat. I tried the coat on and I imagined how good it would look on my mom, so I bought it for her Christmas present.

This is the first time since I left home that I am in the Christmas spirit. Usually, I would spend Christmas at the shelter for battered women and donate five hundred dollars to help the women and their kids. I still will be donating the money but I plan to spend this Christmas with my parents.

Chapter Eight: Office Christmas Party

The office Christmas party is next Friday. I might as well shop for an outfit since I am already out at the mall. I know I have to look good. The accountant firm invited their clients to the party as well as every employee. I am looking forward to seeing all of the accountant firm clients. This is my first office party that I will be attending. I know we work for the mayor's office, teacher's union, doctor's offices, and many other companies.

It's Saturday morning the day of the Christmas party. It is almost time to get dress. I am not rushing to get dressed because I had already laid my clothes out on the bed. I imagined how good I was going to look when I got dressed. I took a shower and got dressed. I looked at myself in a full-length mirror and damn I do not remember the last time I looked this good.

Well, I guess it was when I went to the hospital ball with Jason two years ago. Only this time, I am going to wear what I want to wear. I had on a long light blue dress with the splits on both sides half way up my thighs. The front and back had a v-neckline. I had bought myself a blue sapphire diamond necklace and earrings to match. Who said that a man had to buy a woman diamonds? I was not going to the party with a man. I did not want to go with a man. Although plenty of men asked to take me; I turned them all down. At this point in my life, I do not want a man.

I wore my hair half in a French roll and I let the back hang down. I had gotten my nails done and had doves painted on all of them to represent the year of my freedom. I love every moment of it. I am so proud of myself and all of my accomplishments.

When I walked into that Christmas party, I know that all eyes are going to be on me when I step in that room. I know I look good. Just as I figured, as I walked in the room everyone was starring at me. I could feel their eyes starring at me every time I moved.

I did not care what they thought about me because tonight I feel like a billion dollars. My boss came over to me and said that I was the most beautiful woman at the party and that I looked stunning. He said that he never noticed how beautiful I was. He just knew that I was a good employee. I thanked him for the compliments and walked off.

I had never known my boss to give anyone a good compliment or otherwise. I heard someone say wow you look beautiful as ever. You are the most beautiful and finest woman in the building. I turned around, it was Mr. Wax. He gave me a tight hug. Before he let me go I could feel his hard penis and it reminded me of the old days but I stop myself. I asked him how was his wife doing and was she there at the party. Here she comes headed toward us and I asked him was that his wife and he said yes. She looked nothing as if I had expected she was short and ugly. Why would he pick her over me? He introduced me as one of his students when he had first started teaching.

She then asked me if he was a good teacher. I told her she should know better than anyone if he was a good teacher or not. He took her by the arm and said that he wanted to talk to one of his friends. I watched them walk away. I was just laughing on the inside. I guess the conversation was getting a little too heated for him. I wanted to hear what she was going to say after I had made that comment but he made sure we did not say anything else to each other.

I enjoyed the food and the dancing. I was having a wonderful time. I was getting tired of people telling me how good I looked. The guys acted as if I did not have any mirrors at home. I graciously accepted their compliments anyway and let them know I was not interested in a relationship.

I went over to Tonya and her husband to see if they were having a good time and they were. Tonya and I complemented each other on how good we looked.

It is three o'clock in the morning. I really was not tired but I had not been up that late ever. I was use to being in the bed no later than eleven o' clock p.m. I went over to Judy and told her I had a great time and I was leaving. She asked me if I wanted her and her date to walk me out to my car. I said no that they should stay and continue to have fun.

I walked over to Tonya and her husband to tell them that I

was calling it a night. They asked me if I wanted them to walk me to the car. I said no, because I did not drink any alcohol. I drunk sprite all night; I just had it put in a wine glass to look like I was drinking champagne.

I was almost to my car when I heard a guy call my name. He said that I was the most beautiful woman on earth. I stopped in my tracks. It felt like my heart had stopped. I got scared and I wanted to scream but I could not. My gun was in my car underneath my seat. As he walked closer to me I was wondering what was he going to do to me. I said to myself calm down he is not going to hurt you. I said to myself that I am not afraid of him and no one else.

I turned around, looked Jason straight in his eyes, and said thanks for the compliment. He asked how have I been doing and I said great. He asked if I lived back with my parents. I told him that I was not comfortable talking to him about my living arrangements. He said okay. He said Danielle you are still afraid of me and I said no. Do you think that I am going to hurt you? No, I said but I really did not know what to expect from him. He said that he was sorry for beating me up. He said that he had changed and he had gotten some counseling.

I wondered what made him get help. He told me that Dr. Kim convinced him to get help because he had a problem. How did she know you were the one who beat me up? I never told her or the police your name?

He said she had seen us together at the hospital charity ball.

Everyone had noticed how beautiful you were just like tonight. He thanked me for not turning him in to the police and that he was grateful to me. He said that I had given him another chance to make his life better. He gave me a hug, kissed me on the cheek, and said that he would always love me until he dies. He opened my car door for me and I got in the car.

On the way home, I kept looking in my rearview mirror and my side mirrors to make sure that no one was following me home. What a great night. I had fun dancing and the food was good too. On top of that, Jason had apologized to me, and he seemed to be very sincere. I could not be more pleased with the way my life had turned out. Who would have thought that I would become a supervisor at a top accountant firm?

I never thought I could live without a man in my life or live this long without sex. It has been two years since I had sex. I have decided that I will not have sex again until I get married.

Chapter Nine: Christmas Day

It is Christmas day and I am feeling good just a little nervous. I plan to visit my parents today whether they want to see me or not. It has been three years and I think it is time to see them. I must be the bigger person. I know that I can ask them to forgive me because I know my mom's pride would not let her ask me for forgiveness first, even if she is a Christian.

I realized that I hurt her but I could not stay a child forever. I am really looking forward to seeing everyone. I want see their faces when I give them their gifts.

I was not expecting them to give me anything, since they do not know I am coming over. I hope my mom is fixing all of my favorite dishes. I have not cooked since I left Jason.

I wonder how my parents will react to seeing me at their front door. Will they be happy to see me or will they tell me to go back to my home? I had already made up my mind that this is going to be the best Christmas ever no matter what happens over to my parent's house.

It is three o' clock and I am loading all of the gifts into my car. By the time, I got to the house I just sat in my car trying to get my nerves together to walk up to the door.

When I got to the door, David opened the door before I could ring the doorbell. I would have had to put something down first before I could ring the doorbell; since my hands are full with presents. I stepped inside the door and he took some of the presents out of my hands. He put them on the floor. He picked me up and turned me around like he use to do when we were kids. He told me that this was the best Christmas he has had in three years. He put me down, my other two brothers came over and gave me a hug. They told me that they were proud of me to have enough nerves to face our parents.

They said that they have missed me so much and they were glad to see me. My dad came over, gave me a hug, turned me around in the air, and said that he missed me and it was about time that I had come back home. I told him that I missed him too. He said welcome back home my beautiful daughter. What he said made me feel very special. He is the only man in my life who never lied to me.

My mom just stared at me. I did not know how to read that look on her face. I did not know if she was happy to see me or if she wanted me to leave her house. Then she said can I get a hug too or is the hugs just for the guys. I ran over to her and gave her a great big bear hug. I told her that I was sorry for the way I left home. I kissed her on the cheek and told her that I really missed her and that I wanted her to be in my life for as long as we lived.

She told me that she missed me and we will always keep in touch for now on. We sat down and ate dinner. My brothers and I talked about the good ole days, when we were little kids and all the fun things we use to do together. My brothers cleaned up while my parents and I talked. Mom asked me if I was still with Jason. I told her no we had broken up two years ago. I did not elaborate on how we broken up because I know my brothers would hunt him down.

I told them that I had gone to college and my job had paid for it. Now I am a supervisor at the accountant firm where I work.

They were so proud of me they said that they knew I would make something special out of my life. I told them that I live in a one-bedroom apartment, I like it, they would have to come and visit me one day. They said that they would come and see my apartment.

The doorbell rung and my brother said Danielle the door is for you. I looked at my parents and said that I wondered who could be at the door because I did not tell anyone I was coming over here.

I went to the door and I was surprised, that it was Jason. I asked him what was he doing here and how did he know I was here.

He asked me how was I doing. I said great. He said he saw my car in the drive way and he was on his way to his friend's house who lived down the street from my parents. He asked if it was a bad time to talk to me. I said no. We stayed on the porch. I did not feel right to invite him in my parent's house after what had happened the last time he was here.

He said he wanted to talk to me and see how I was doing since the party. He wanted me to meet his friend so we walked over to his car. He said Danielle this is Carl. Carl this is Danielle. I shook Carl's hand and said glad to meet you but on the inside I was about to gag but I held my composer. I was shocked and could not believe that Jason's friend was a guy. He walked me back to the house. He kissed me on the cheek and said Merry Christmas. I told him Merry Christmas, and I hope he was happy.

He walked back to his car and I was going in the house. He said wait, he forgot that he had something for me. I told him that he did not have to give me anything because I did not buy him anything. He gave me the diamond necklace and earrings that he had given me for the hospital ball a couple years ago. He said that they belong to me.

At first I did not want to take them but I thought to myself what would Carl do with them. Besides, they look better on me anyways. I took the diamonds from him. It would be the end of that relationship and closure for the both of us. We hugged good-bye and he left.

I went back inside of the house and I begin to trip about how could he be gay and I did not know it? I guess I should have known that a straight guy did not keep his place so clean and so organized. Carl must have been the guy who called to see how Jason was doing the day he lost his first patient. He also must have been the person who would call and hang up on me whenever I answered the phone.

Why did I have to be the first woman Jason had to sex with? I hope I do not have aids. The first thing that I am going to do on

Monday is take an aids test.

I stayed a little while longer and visited with my family because I was enjoying their company. I finally went home and I could not grasp the fact that Jason was gay. All of the signs were there and I did not see any of them.

Chapter Ten: Nervous About Test

I could not wait until the next day, so I could call Tonya up and tell her about Jason. They had moved and bought a house, so I know they did not keep in contact with the people in that apartment anymore.

When I told her about Jason, she did not seem to be surprised. She said that she knew something was wrong with him. Before I moved in with him she never seen him with any woman. I told her that I was going to work late on Monday because I wanted to go to the doctor to be tested, to make sure that I did not have aids. I went to the doctor's office and I was scared I was sweating bullets waiting to see the doctor and when he came into the exam room, I told him I wanted to be tested for aids. He told me to calm down and relax that his nurse would draw some blood. The test results would be back in about two weeks.

At work, I would think about the test results. The two weeks went by slow and Tonya had to keep reassuring me that everything was going to be okay.

My mom had called me and asked me to go to church with her on Sunday, to their family and friend day. I said okay. I had not been to church in so long. I did not want to go by myself so I called

Tonya and asked if she and her husband could go to church with me on Sunday. They said yes. The church service was good but the program was too long for me but I needed all the prayers I could get.

The doctor called me Monday evening. He told me that the test was negative but I should follow up the test in about six months. I am sure he said that I did not have the aids virus. I was so happy. I started jumping up and down screaming thank you Jesus real loud. I didn't care if my neighbors thought I was crazy or not. I was so happy that I didn't have aids.

After the shock had worn off, I sat down on the couch and just thought back over my life. I thought about how many times I came close to death. I am truly blessed. I realized that this is my life and I will live it the way I want. I will not take anything for granted. I will do whatever it takes to make my life happier for now and forever. I will always keep in touch with my family and I will never let a man ever come between me and my family. I will not get involved with a man when my instinct is telling me that something is wrong with a guy. I am happier than I've ever been. I do not have a man in my life right now and that is my choice.

I love the way my life has turned out and I would not change anything. I just know that I would never stay in an abusive relationship again. I chalked that experience up as a test that I passed with flying colors. All I can say is that this is my life and I will live my life the way I want.

Although I love my life, I had decided to back to college and get a bachelor degree in accounting. I wanted to get a better job and maybe one day I could be my own boss. Things at work are getting a little crazy. My boss hired his son to run things and to me his job was to make everyone miserable. I hate to go to work now because he was always changing the way we did things. If he did not like you, he would fire you.

Everyone loved their lunchtime. We felt like we were back in high school and the best part of school was lunch. When I first decided to go, back to college I was a little nervous. I felt out of place because most of the students were eighteen years old. Here I was twenty-one years old. I am determined to graduate because I want a better job.

I must admit that the kids thought it was great for me to go back to school. They loved having me as a study partner. I guess they just assumed that I was smart. I thought it was great they accepted me into their study group. By me working during the day their support makes going back to college easier for me. I have not had a steady boyfriend since Jason. I am not ready for a serious relationship at least not until I achieve all of my goals first.

Besides, I promised myself that I do not want to have sex anymore, until I get married. I thought that it would be hard for me not to have sex. It seems as if I do not have a desire for sex anymore. I do not know what is wrong with me but I love what has happened to me.

I always look forward to Saturdays because I go over to Tonya's house and play cards every weekend. I just get tired of them trying to fix me up with a blind date. They just do not get it that I do not want a man in my life right now. I know Tonya wants me to be happily married like her but it not meant to be for me right now. Why do people think your life is not complete if you are not married and have children? All I want to do is get my life together before I have anyone else in my life.

Tonya called me today and said that she was pregnant. She is having mixed emotions right now. I told her that she would be a great mother because she is a terrific friend. She asked me to be the godmother. I happily said yes. I said I cannot wait to spoil my godchild.

Tonya said that she wants a girl because you can dress little girls better than you can boys. I hope she has a little boy because I had all brothers. I knew what boys liked more than girls do, although I was a little girl once.

Tonya said that she wished we could be pregnant together so she would not have to do it alone. I thought to myself that she must be crazy I do not want any kids.

I was glad that Tonya and I are still best friends after three years. I do not know what I would have done without her in my life. She has always had my back since she saved me from Jason. Sometimes even when I don't want to hear what she has to say; she always gives me good advice and encourages me. She is like the sister I never had. My family has adopted her and her husband as part of our family.

They go with me to my parent's house on every holiday.

Tonya and I love to go on shopping sprees once a month and we shop until we drop. Tonya likes to look at everything even things she knows she would not buy. By the time I gets home I am exhausted and ready for some sleep, after I soak my feet. I love shopping but I guess after the baby gets here we will not do as much shopping. I am looking forward to shopping for the baby.

Chapter Eleven: The Unfortunate Event

It is close for Tonya to have the baby. She has three weeks before the baby is born. My phone is ringing and it is three o'clock in the morning. I am thinking that Tonya must be ready to have her baby, so I answered the phone and said hello. At first, no one said anything then a man's voice said hello. My name is Carl and I do not know if you remember me. I am Jason's friend. He was shot today, and he just asked me to call you because he needs to see you. We are at Sullivan's Hospital. He hung up the phone. I got dressed and went to the hospital.

On the way there, I was wondering why Jason wanted to see me after all of these years. Why would someone shoot him and how did it happen? I guess I would find out the answer to these questions when I get to the hospital.

When I arrived at the hospital, Carl met me down the hallway. He walked me to Jason's room. On the way to his room, Carl told me that someone had broken into their apartment and shot Jason. Why didn't they shoot Carl too? I thought to myself. I guess I should not ask him that question right now. However, I did ask him why Jason wanted to see me? It has been two years since I last saw him. Carl said that he had no idea why he wanted to see me. From the expression on his face he did not seem to be happy that Jason had asked to see me.

The doctor came out of the room and asked me if my name was Danielle. I said yes. He said that Jason was asking for me and that I could go in to see him but not to stay long because he was weak from the surgery.

I walked in the room. He laid there as if he was already dead. He had wires and tubes everywhere. From a distance, he did not look anything like himself. He was very skinny and he looked like an old man. He looked like he was in his fifties instead of his late thirties. I walked closer to him and I asked him how he was feeling. He said that he did not have much time. He told me that he loved me more than anyone in his life. He said that He was sorry for the way he treated me and I made him a better person. He asked me to forgive him. I had forgiven him years ago but I guess he needed to hear me say it again. I told him that I forgive him. He reached for my hand so I held his hand tight. He told me not to trust Carl. He had a frown on his face, so I squeezed his hand tighter. I promised him that I would never trust Carl and he smiled.

The machine started making noises, the nurses and doctors rushed into the room. The nurse asked me to leave. Carl asked me what was going on. I told him that Jason was not going to make it.

A few seconds later, the doctor came out and told us that Jason had died. Carl started acting like a fool yelling and screaming from the top of his lungs. No, No, No! You cannot leave me! I love you so much! He fell on his knees saying God you cannot take him away from me. It seemed like he was fake crying. I did not know what to do to help him so I just watched him act a fool, until a nurse asked him if she could call someone for him.

Jason's Mom asked me what did her son wanted with me. I

told her that I would talk to her later. She said okay. I asked her if she needed me to stay there with her and she said yes. After they took his body to the funereal home, we left Carl there at the hospital. He was still acting a fool when we went home.

I remembered that Jason asked me not to trust him. I felt sorry for Jason even though he was dead. I was sad and confused as to why he asked me not to trust Carl.

Carl had asked me what Jason had said to me.
I said he asked me to forgive him. What business was it for him to know what we talked about? He seemed to be acting very strange to me.

It was almost time for work, so I got dressed and went to work. I was so tired I did not want to be at work but I had to meet with an important client today.

At lunch I called Tonya and told her what had happen to Jason and she was freaking out. I told her I thought she was calling me to tell me that she was about to have the baby.

She said that she wish the baby would hurry up and come because she is tired of carrying the heavy load.

Finally, the work day is over. I was glad to go to class and concentrate on my finals. While I took the finals, it got my mind off Jason for a while. I felt very good about my exams.

Today is Jason's funeral and I have so many mixed emotions. True enough I had forgiven him but I still wondered why he chose me to date, when he knew he was gay. Why did he choose to date me out of all the women he worked with?

When I got to the funeral, his mother asked me to come and sit with her so I did. We always got along well. Now I know why she was so happy that Jason and I were dating. I guess she always wanted him to be straight.

After I left the cemetery, I went home and got into bed. My brother David called me and asked how I was doing? He said he was sorry that he could not go with me to the funeral. He said that he could not get the day off work. He said it had to be awkward for me to be at Jason's funeral. He said that if I needed anything to call him. I said thanks for the support and that the funeral was not that bad.

Tonya called me about thirty minutes later and asked how was I doing? I told her that I was okay. She asked me if there were many gay people there. I told her I did not know who all was gay or not. The only person I know for sure was gay is Carl.

She laughed and said that if she was there she could pick out every gay person there. She did not go with me because she said that it would not be good for the baby and besides she did not like Jason anyways.

She could never forgive him for the way he treated me.

Chapter Twelve: Drama

The next day I was at work when Michael Hummington called me. He told me that he was Jason's attorney and he needed to see me today at five thirty.

I got to his office at five thirty exactly. Mrs. Taylor (Jason's mother) and Carl was already there waiting on me. I sat between the two of them. The attorney read Jason's will as follow:

He leaves to his mother his black Porsche, stocks and bonds. He leaves Danielle Hudson then he paused---two million dollars. My mouth flew open I was shocked. I did not know that he had that kind of money.

The next thing we knew Carl had fainted and fell out of his chair. He laid on the floor and Mrs. Taylor and I just looked at him laying there. Neither one of us bothered to help him or to see if he was all right.

The Attorney called his secretary to bring him some water. After he helped him into his chair; he asked Carl if he was all right. He said yes.

He then continues to tell Carl that he could have all of the clothes but Ms. Hudson and Mrs. Taylor could pick out the pieces of jewelry first.

Carl started to ranting and raving saying that it was a joke. He knew that Jason would not leave a b----- two million dollars because he loves me and not that b-------. He kept calling me a b------ and I was getting ticked off and I was about to kick his butt but Mrs. Taylor was holding my hand. She asked me not to do anything crazy. I have respect for my elders, so I did not act a fool and go off on his stupid behind.

The attorney told Carl to stop acting like a crazy fool in his office or else he was going to call security. Carl calmed down. The attorney said that Jason you would act like that, so he left you this.

He handed Carl a letter. He snatched it out of his hand and stormed out of the office like he was a little school girl having a tantrum. He told me that the money was already deposit into my account this morning.

The three of us all walked out to our cars together. Out of nowhere, a car tried to run us over and I barely got out of the way of the car. We got a good look at the car. We knew that it was Carl driving the car, although we did not see his face.

I told Mr. Hummington and Mrs. Taylor that the day Jason died he asked me not to trust or believe Carl.

I did not know exactly what that meant but I do now. It is beginning to make sense.

What if an intruder did not shot Jason but instead it was

Carl? How could we prove that he killed Jason?

Mr. Hummington said, we should call the police and let them handle it. After we tell them everything we know.

After the police investigated the case, they found out that Carl did shoot Jason.

Carl had a gambling habit. He owed his bookie a lot of money. He thought that Jason had left all of his money to him.

Chapter Thirteen: A New Beginning

The day Carl was sentenced Mrs. Taylor and I was there. We were happy that the judge had given him life in prison, without parole.

Good that is where he belongs. He would fit in perfectly. Getting my bachelor degree in accounting came in handy with the two million dollar I received. It has taken my life to a completely new level. I can now become my own boss. No one can tell me what to do or threaten to fire me ever again.

Tonya and I went looking for the perfect building for my new office. We found the perfect place downtown. It was a two story brick building with glass windows you could see into the first floor. I brought the place and named my company Hudson C.P.A. Company.

The first floor consists of a coffee shop and a newspaper stand.

Judy and a few of my ex co-workers came to work for me. because they were sick of the new management as well.

I had hired the best vice president in the world. I did not hire Ed because Tonya and I were best friends. I hired him because I felt he was responsible enough to do the job. Also he was responsible for me getting into accounting in the first place. He had years of experience in accounting and management. Besides, I trust Ed with my life. He had saved my life once already.

I know that I did not have to go to work every day because Ed and Judy was capable handling everything without me anyways.

I would have hired Tonya but since she had Ed Jr., she did not want to work anymore.

I can remember when I first met Tonya she did not want any children. The day she gave birth to Ed Jr. she scared me to death.

When she was in labor she was hollering and screaming. Oh shoots this hurts! Give me something to knock me out! She had poor Ed confused. One minute she would tell him to get out of her face and better yet get out of this room.

When it was time for the baby to come out, she had Ed to come back into the room.

I asked her when is she going to give me another godchild. She looks at me crazy and said; you must what me to kick your butt. I do not want to go through that type of pain again.

She is a great mother. At first she had her doubts about being a mother. It has been three years since Jason had died and the time seems to have flown by. I can remember how long its been since Jason died because Ed Jr., was born two weeks later. I often go to Jason's grave and put a dozen of fresh red roses on his grave.

After Jason's death, Mrs. Taylor, my mother and I meet every second Saturday of every month and have dinner. I looked forward to spending time with these two wonderful older women.

A funny thing happened to my mom. She and Mrs. Taylor became best friends. I was happy for my mom because she finally had a best friend. She has someone who she could spend some time with shopping and having fun besides getting on my dad's last nerves.

However, I hated that they would gain up on me about getting married and having children. I would tell them when the right man comes along the two of them would be the first to know.

I have not had a man in my life in years. Yes, I have had a few booty calls but only when I needed to satisfying my sexual desire which was not that often.

I will wait for Mr. Right to have sex. I refuse to let another man walk all over my heart, as if I do not have feelings. I am in control of my life . I love the way I live my life.

Chapter Fourteen: Ten Year Class Reunion

Wow, what a feeling. I feel like I am on top of the world. I have achieved most of my goals in life.

Next week is my ten-year class reunion. I am really looking forward to seeing my old friends. I am looking forward to seeing everyone even the people that I did not like. I even looked forward to seeing the people who did not like me. It will be interesting to see how much everyone has changed. I regret not keeping in touch with the group of girls I use to hang around. I never ran into anyone I went to school with, after High School.

What happened to them? I know everybody could not have moved out of town. I wondered what Mr. Wax had been doing? Would he be at the class reunion along with some of the other teachers?

I hope he is there. I feel like that relationship has never been resolved. For some reason I need closure from that relationship and I don't know why.

I wondered if he still looked the same, or have he gained some weight. If he is still married and have any kids.

I know that I should not give a damn about him. I am curious to find out for the last time, if he had an affair with Jan. I was not going to let him get away with lying to me. I do not know what I am going to do if I find out that he did have an affair with her. I do not know why it bugs me so much after all these years. I am going to tell him that I busted him. I saw Jan with my own two eyes.

I cannot wait to see those two in action I am going to be watching their every move. Jan was the most popular girl in our class. She was a cheerleader and all of the boys liked her. She hung out with the most popular girls. She was definitely stuck on herself. She was a nice looking girl but she did not look better than I did. I am not bragging on my looks.

She was the opposite of me. She had big breast and a flat butt with little hips. She had short hair but she always kept it looking nice. You could not tell her anything, because she knew she was the finest girl that ever lived.

Tonya and I went shopping to find me a stunning dress. The dress had to be perfect. I wanted it to show my shape off, with all of it curves.

When I was in school, I had no curves or breast I was a thirty-two a cup and now I am a thirty-six d cup. I wanted everyone who teased me, both guys and girls to look at me and eat their hearts out when they see me enter into the room.

I wanted them to know that my breast was real and I had no breast implants.

What can I say after looking at thousands of dresses I manage to find the perfect dress? It is a red dress with the hemline just a little below my knees. It looked like I had legs for days. The neckline was in a v-shape. My breast was showing but in good taste.

I made sure that if I danced I would not have a breast malfunction. I did not have any splits in my dress because I figured that my low neckline was enough for them to focus on. I wore a diamond necklace, with a dove made of diamonds hanging on it, with matching earrings and a tennis bracelet made of doves.

I brought some satin red shoes and a purse to match the dress perfectly. When I got dressed, I stood in the full-length mirror and made sure everything was in place.

Tonya was their giving me support. When I came out of the bedroom, she said damn girl you look good. It is a good thing that I am not gay. With her approval, I was ready to head to the class reunion.

I decided to drive my black on black convertible jaguar.

When I walked into the banquet hall there were people sitting at almost all of the tables. All three hundred students must be here.

The first person to come over to me was my best friend in high school. Kim and I exchanged hugs and fake kisses. We told each other how good we looked. She took me back to the table where she was sitting. All of our old gang was sitting together. As usual we were fooling around and talking about everyone; how they were still dressing the same way they did in high school.

We blazed on people hairstyles and on the people who was

real skinny then and now they are bigger than two houses.

Scott came over to me and said hi to me. I really had no idea who he was. He told me that he used to be lead starter on the basketball team. I thought to myself Oh, my God what had happened to him? He used to be so fine. Every girl wanted him for a boyfriend. Now he is so out of shape and he seems to be a little shorter. Looking at him was hard to believe. I use to have a crush on him from kindergarten through the twelfth grade.

Sam came over and talked to me. It was hard to imagine he was as a nerd back in the day. He was so fine now. He asked me to dance with him. I was rather hesitant because he was there with his wife. I told him that I would dance with him only if his wife says it is okay. As we danced together, I noticed Mr. Wax and his wife on the dance floor. It was hard to miss him since he bumped into us. I acted as if I did not notice him.

I went back to my seat, a little while later Mr. Wax came over, and we talked for a while. He told me how good I looked and that he thinks about me everyday. He said the biggest mistake that he ever made was not marrying me. I did not know that he had ever asked me to marry him. What in the world is he talking about?

He just did not know that for me, not marrying him was the best thing that ever happened to me.

He had gained a little weight. He was bald headed, and his head was shinning. You could practically see yourself. He was still fine as ever with his mannish smile and sexy dimples.

While we were talking, miss thing finally made her

appearance with a sexy man on her arm.

He was so fine, if he was butter he would have melted all ready.

Jan looked the same she had gained about twenty pounds but it looked good on her. However, she still had a flat butt. She seemed to spot Mr. Wax and me.

They were heading toward us and I was going to the bathroom and Mr. Wax was about to go back to his wife.

She said Hi Danielle and before I could say hi to her, she was hugging Mr. Wax. She acted as if her date and I was not standing there.

I was checking out Mr. Wax's face and his posture. He looked nervous as if he had something to hide. He looked very guilty.

I thought it was rude of Jan not to introduce her date to anyone.

I went to the bathroom and left them talking. I did not have to use the bathroom. I just wanted to make sure my makeup and clothes was fitting right.

When I returned to my table Jan and her date was sitting at our table. I was surprised to see Jan sitting at our table since she was not in our click in high school.

Jan was sitting in the seat next to me on the right side. If she was going to sit at our table, she should have sat directly across from me, so I could have enjoyed looking at her date.

I thought when I sat down she would change seats with her

date but she did not. I wanted to ask her if she had an affair with Mr. Wax when we were in high school but I did not ask her.

A guy came over and asked me to dance. We danced a couple of songs. On the way, back to my seat Mr. Wax approached me again and asked me to dance. I said only if your wife says okay. He told me that he did not need to ask his wife's permission to dance with anyone.

I figured that this would be the perfect time to confront him. I asked him if he had an affair with Jan. He said that he never slept with her. I told him that on graduation day I saw her come to his house and leave.

He swore to me that it was not Jan. It was his roommate's friend. I cannot believe that after all these years; he can still look me in my face and lie to me again.

That settles it he is still a big liar. I hate liars. I need to get far away from him as I can before I go off on him. I left him on the dance floor. I went back to my seat.

When I got back to the table, Jan had switched seats with her date. He was now sitting next to me. She got up to talk to her friends who used to be snobs in school.

I introduced myself to her date. I told him that my name is Danielle. He said that his name was Barry Wilson. I introduced him to everyone at the table.

Jan cannot be wrapped to tight because who in their right mind would leave a fine brother like that. It was obvious that she did not have any manners because she did not introduce Barry to anyone.

She paid more attention to Mr. Wax than she did to Barry. I asked him how long have they been dating? He said that they are not dating. He just met her yesterday.

He had enough of her and he was about to leave. I convinced him to stay. He said that Jan had no class or manners. I decided to leave that one alone.

He asked me to dance and we did. I knew that it would probably make Jan mad but I did not care since she was not paying him any attention anyway.

When we got back to the table, she said that I must like her leftovers. I told her since Barry is not dating her and nor have he slept with her he is not her leftover. She sat back down next to me and Barry sat on the other side of me.

I could tell she was mad because she had her arms folded and she poked her lips out. She asked me if Mr. Wax and I had anything going on.

None of your business I told her. She said that we seemed to be more than student and teacher relationship going on and I looked her directly into her eyes and told her to mind her own damn business and leave mines alone.

I asked her why she wants to know what my relationship is with Mr. Wax. She said because he used to be my man in high school. If I want him now he will still be my man. She said while you little girls were messing with the boys your age, I was sleeping with Mr. Wax.

I am thinking oh the truth finally came out but let me burst miss thing bubble.

I told her you know how you said that I like your leftovers; well you are the one who likes my leftovers.

Everyone at the table was in shock at this shy little quiet girl and what I was talking about. I told her on the day of graduation when she came over to Mr. Wax house I was there.

She had a stupid look on her face. She looked like she was so humiliated and embarrassed. If you are all, of that why did he send you home? You looked liked a little lost puppy dog that night.

She got up from the table and ran out to her car. Kim and everyone at our table were laughing so hard. She finally got what she deserved. Now she got a chance to see what it feels like to be humiliated.

Was I a bad person for going off on her in front of everyone? I do not feel sorry for her because she use to hurt my feelings many of times. I guess that is why payback is a MF.

I enjoyed the rest of the night. All of us girls danced with Barry. He did not care that Jan had left him. He knew that someone would take him home.

Barry and I danced so much. I had not had that much fun in a long time. After the reunion, all of the people at our table went to a restaurant.

Barry rode to the restaurant with me. I enjoyed the conversation. He was a very intelligent man. At the restaurant we all ordered different meals. We tried everything on each other plates. We laughed and talked about Jan. We had so much fun. Kim and I vowed to keep in touch with each other, even though she lives in another state.

I took Barry home and he invited me to come in but I declined. I did not know him well enough to go inside. Besides, I had been down that road before. I promised myself that I would not make the same mistake twice.

We exchanged cell phone numbers. He said that he was going to call me. When I got home, I was so tired. I could barely get my clothes off. I have not slept this good ever.

Chapter Fifteen: Surprise of My Life

It Sunday and I did not get out of the bed until two o'clock in the evening. I can get used to sleeping in on Sunday.

I am living a wonderful life and I love the way I live.

It is six o'clock in the evening and someone is ringing my doorbell. I went to the door and it was a chauffer. He said that I needed to come with him. I asked him who had sent for me. He told me that it was a surprise and he could not tell me.

He took me to the airport. I got on a private plane and it was beautiful inside. It looked like an expensive living room with a bar.

It even had a chandelier in the middle of the dining table. The pilot and the flight attendant came in to greet me. I asked them who owned the plane and where are they taking me?

The pilot said that it was a surprise. They could not give me more information than that. The pilot went back to the cockpit and the flight attendant told me to fasten my seatbelt.

I called Tonya and told her that I was on a private airplane. I did not know where I was going. I did not know who was behind all of this. I wanted Tonya to know that nothing terrible had happened to me.

It seemed like we were in the air for at least six hours. We landed in the middle of nowhere. I did not see any houses, just trees everywhere. They opened the door and there was a jaguar limousine waiting for me.

The chauffeur opened the door for me. Before I could ask him where he was taking me, he had closed the door. He did not drive far before I saw a beautiful huge castle. I had seen that castle so many times before in my dreams when I was little.

I guess I always wanted to be a princess when I grew up. The chauffeur opens the door and lets me out of the car. I walked slowly up to the door. The scenery of the trees and the garden were beautiful.

I loved the sound of the water falling from the waterfall. The water was a crisp white. It was relaxing just looking at the water.

I have always loved the sound of water. When I got to the front door, the butler opened it before I could knock on the door.

The suspense was killing me. I could not wait to see who had summoned me to this beautiful place.

A servant came and she took me up to my bedroom. She opened the door and there are no words to describe this beautiful room.

On the bed lied a beautiful long black gown. I had never seen anything like it. It must have cost at least two hundred thousand dollars or more. There was a tiara lying at the head of the dresser.

Another servant came in to help me get dress. When I was finished, she put a black diamond necklace and earrings on me. I looked like a real princess. I felt like a princess.

She told me to follow her down the stairs. She then instructed me to wait until she got on the last step. I followed her instructions and I took my time going down the stairs. I was looking too beautiful to fall down the stairs.

When I got to the last step I did not see anyone but the servants. They led me to the dining room. That was the longest dining table I had ever seen except for on television. The china was white trimmed in gold around the edge of the china. The crystal glasses was also trimmed in gold. The silverware was made of gold. The centerpieces were made of white lilies that was dipped in gold. Everything was so gorgeous.

The servant showed me where to sit. I sat next to the head of the table. I looked around to see if I could see the person who had summoned me here but I did not see anyone.

I know whomever this man is he knew me very well. He knew that I liked water, beautiful clothes not to mention that everything fit me to the t.

The suspense is killing me I cannot stand not knowing who this person is. Finally, I see a man in a black tuxedo coming towards me.

I cannot see his face yet. He is getting closer and I cannot believe my eyes.

He stands about six feet and seven inches. I cannot wait until he gets close so I can see his face. He came over to me. He took me by the hand and lifted me to my feet.

He gave me a hug, and then he kissed me. I was astonished

and I cannot believe that he would go through all of this for me. I was too lost for words. I was happy to see him. I was so happy that I begin to cry.

I finally met the man of my dreams. I am in love with him and I cannot describe the feeling. I just know that he is the Mr. Right.

We ate dinner and we did not say much we just ate and stared at each other like we were both inside of my dream.

After dinner, he took me into the ballroom and we slow danced for hours. As we danced, I felt like we were one person instead of two separate people.

I needed someone to pinch me because this whole day has been, as if I am in a dream. I asked him how he knew so much about me. He said Jason was his best friend and while they were at the gym Jason always talked a lot about me. He knew what type a woman I was. That is how he knew everything I liked.

He said that it was time for a man to treat me like the princess that I am. He told me that the first time he laid eyes on me he knew that he was in love with me and that he was going to marry me. He said that he wanted to erase all of my pain and make me complete again.

He wanted to give me the world, although I had my own business and millions. He wants me to love life to the fullest and that could not happen until I marry him.

I never thought a man could ever sweep me off my feet but he sure did. What made it so good is that I never seen it coming.

I knew Mr. Right was out there but I did not expect to meet him so soon. I feel like my life has come to a full circle.

I should have known it was him. The day I met him I had a feeling that we were made for each other, because we connected right away.

We are still dancing and I do not want to stop. I do not know how long we have been dancing but I love being in his arms. I am not thinking about sex. I just want him to hold me.

This is my life, I love the way I live, and I am going to live it with him for the rest of our lives. He walked me up to my bedroom and kissed me at the door and I went in.

I was so happy I never knew happiness could feel so good. I took the tiara off my head and set it on the dresser. I laid in the bed with my dress on and I fell asleep.

The next morning I woke up and I was still in the gown. For some reason I thought if I take the dress off I would wake up and I would have been dreaming.

One of the servants knocked on the door. I told her to come in. She helped me get out of the dress. She gave me some new clothes to put on. As I walked down for breakfast, I realized that I did not know where I was. When I got to the dining room, Michael was waiting for me. I asked him where are we?

He said that we were in Canada. He asked me if I needed to go back home today and I said no but I would need to call Ed and let him know that I am out of town and I will be back in a couple of days if you do not mind me staying. He said that we could stay there as long as we wanted. After breakfast, we went for a walk on the property. This is a beautiful place. How did you ever find this place?

He said after he met me in his office that day, he was looking in a magazine. He said he had to have it because it looked like it was built just for me.

Damn I love this man. He seems to be too good to be true. He knew all the right things to say to me. The look in his eyes let me know that he was sincere about me. I was tired from the walk so I took a nap. When I got up, I had to call my mother because I promised her that when I met Mr. Right I would let her know.

I called her and told her that I had some good news for her. She said that she already knew what I was going to say. She said you are engaged to someone. How did you know? Mrs. Taylor and I knew something was going on when you did not show up for dinner on Saturday. When are we going to met him? When we get back, I will call you and we can set up a date. Will you call Mrs. Taylor and give her the good news? Have you set a date yet? No, I just got engaged last night. You will be the first to know when we set a date.

Michael came in while I was talking to mom. He said your mom must be happy for you. Yes, she had been begging me to get married for years. I cannot wait to talk to Tonya. He said what are you waiting for to call her? I said I was waiting for him to leave. Oh, it is like that. It must be a woman thing. Yes, of course there are some things I do not want you to hear. I hope it is all good? Do not worry it is all-good from beginning to end.

I have not talked to her in seven days so I know she is dying to know what is going on with me. She probably will not believe me when I tell her all about my weekend. I called Tonya, we talked for hours, I gave her every detail, and I did not leave anything out.

She was excited she said we have a wedding to plan. She was so happy, you would think she was getting married all over again.

The next morning we went home. I hated that my dream had to end but I have to get back to reality. I went to the office to show my face and to see how things were going.

Michael came over to my house and a man from the jewelry store brought some engagement rings for us to choose one. They were all beautiful and I could not make up my mind as to which one I wanted. I let Michael pick my ring because he has excellent taste. I told Michael that I do not want a large wedding. I would love to get married in Canada at our castle.

He said that he was counting on getting married there when he brought the place. We seemed to be on the same page as, if we can read each other thought.

He said that he did not believe in long engagements. He asked me to marry him on new years. He wanted to bring the New Year in right with the two of us proclaiming our love with the people we love.

I agreed to marry him on New Years day. That means that I have six months to plan the wedding. I know how I want it done so I hired a wedding planner. Tonya and I loved to shop but I told her that I was having my wedding gown made. She helped me design the gown and the veil.

Michael and I agreed not to have sex until our wedding day. It was easy for me since I had not had sex in years. Michael and I have so much in common, and it was unbelievable. I love him so much that I cannot put it into word to describe how I feel about him.

I love my life and now it seems to be complete with him by my side. Both of our businesses are doing very good and we do not have to worry about money. The only thing we had to do was get through the wedding.

Everybody was excited that I was getting married. They all wanted to play some type of part in the wedding. I made it clear that I did not want a large wedding but an elegant wedding.

We were just having the best man, matron of honor, ring bearer, and a flower girl. I did not want a long drawn out ceremony.

It seems like everyone wanted me to have this huge wedding. They said that I had waited a long time so I should do it big. I had to tell them that this is Michael's and my wedding. We are doing it our way.

Chapter Sixteen: Christmas Time

It is Christmas day; we went over to my parent's house for dinner. Everyone there was going to be at our wedding. I loved the fact that Michael and my family got along. It was as if our families had known each other for a long time.

We love each other and respect everyone. Mom and Mrs. Taylor did all of the cooking and the food was delicious. We sat around talking about the good ole days. We had so much fun, until I could not wait for all of us to get together again for our wedding.

A week to go before the wedding and I was calm. I did not have any running around to do. That would not have been possible if I did not have the wedding planner. She was wonderful. She did everything, including making sure that the designer had my gown ready two weeks before the wedding.

I would have my last fitting the day before the wedding. Michael took care of decorating the castle. He said that he wanted to make it special for me.

That is one thing I loved about him. He always put me first. I always put him first. It is the day of the wedding and everything is going smoothly.

I had to stay in my room all day but that was not a problem it was so beautiful. I went out on the Terrance for air.

I had plenty of people to keep me company until midnight. Mom and Mrs. Taylor thought that I should have stayed at a hotel. Why waste money when this house was so huge there was know way I would run into Michael.

It is three hours until the wedding and I was getting my hair done, makeup, manicure, and pedicure at the same time. I was hoping they would be finish so I could have some alone time before a walked down that long stairway.

I was not nervous I just needed the time to myself. It was just too much going on in here. They got finished and helped me get dressed and everyone left the room accepted mom. She told me how proud she was of all of my accomplishment that I have made in my life. She said that she loves me and has always wanted the best for me. She asked me to forgive her for being mean to me the day I left home. We hugged and I told her that I forgive her and I hope she forgives me for the way I had behaved that day.

She started to cry and said my baby has grown up. You look stunning. You are the most beautiful bride I have ever seen. I started crying. My mother had never given me a compliment nor had she told me that she loved me.

I had to get my face touchup because my mascara was running down my face. It is Showtime, the music is playing, and someone knocked on my door and opened it for me.

I was more than ready to become Mrs. Michael

Hummington. I loved the way that sounded Danielle Hummington. I walked to the stairs and proceeded slowly down the stairs carrying a dozen of purple orchids. My gown was made of silk; it was white with real diamonds around the collar of the gown, which laid off my shoulders. I had long sleeves made of silk lace and it flared at the end of my arms.

The gown fitted my body until it got to my waist and it flared out like the dresses in the eighteen hundreds. The train and the veil were thirty feet long. The veil consisted of a silk lace as well and I had my face covered.

As I walked down the stairs, I reminisced about the last time, I walked down the stairs and I felt like a princess. Today I feel like a queen. I feel beautiful and I could not wait to get to the alter to see Michael.

I did not know that I could be so happy. When I got to the bottom step, my dad was waiting for me and he looked gorgeous. He told me that I looked beautiful and that he loved me. He said that he approved of Michael. He loved him as if he was his son and he knows that Michael will make me happy.

I almost started to cry again but I held back the tears. It seemed like it took me forever to get up there to Michael. He was so handsome. I just wanted the preacher to pronounce us man and wife, so we could leave and get busy.

The ceremony was short and sweet. He introduced us as Mr. and Mrs. Michael Hummington and we kissed. I knew that I was the luckiest woman in the world. I cannot express how much I love my life. I am now Danielle Hummington and I love my husband. This is our life and we love the way we are going to live it happily, in love forever.

It's My Life

My life is so boring; I can barely stand it,
I feel as if I have the weight,
of the world lying on my shoulders.
The heaviness of my problems is holding me down.

Sometimes I feel distraught, like there is nothing,
or no one to lift up my spirit.
It seems like no one can help me get back on my feet.

I wonder which way is my life headed.
Is success lying straight ahead, or is there a dead end,
lurking around the corner waiting for me?

My life seems so dark,
I don't have anyone to spend my life with.
Who can I share my life with?
Who can I give all of this love, I have
Stored up inside of me?

Is there a man who can hold me close, and comfort me?
Can he give me the kind, of love that I so richly deserve?
Can he satisfy me and make my life complete?

I know the difference between right, wrong, good, and bad.
I must make the ultimate decision
that will put my life on the right path.
I know that I am the only one that has destiny over my own life.

I will live my life to the fullest,

just the way I want to.
I won't settle for any old thing,
and certainly not anything that is beneath me.
I will do whatever it takes to make my life happier.
I deserve the best out of life,
and the best is what I will seek.

It' my life and I will live it the way I want!!!!

Created by Evie Brooks

ABOUT THE AUTHOR

Author Evie Brooks is a native of Flint, MI. She has been married for sixteen years. She has four children; three sons and one daughter. She is the third eldest of ten children. She has six sisters and three brothers.

Mrs. Brooks graduated from Davenport University of Flint, MI with a Bachelor Degree in Business Administration.

She is a homemaker and she loves to write. *It's My Life* is her first Romance Novel and she hopes to write and publish many more novels.

Acknowledgments

I would like to give God thanks for giving me the patience and concentration to write *It's My Life*. I would like to give a special thanks to my husband John for being patient with me while, I neglected certain duties around the house. Thanks to my children John II and Jessica, who are also my two biggest fans in the world. I could not have done this book without your support. Thanks for giving me the space I needed to complete this book.

I would like to thank all of my sisters, brothers, nieces, and nephews for all of your support.

I would like to thank La Kesha, Marcus, Sandra, Jackie, Bev Fargo, Dericco, Charmaine, Rachel, Tony Montgomery, Manvel, Molly, Jordyn, Devyn, and Jadyn. Love you all.

I would especially like to give a special thanks to my publisher Florence Dyer. You are a wonderful person who I have enjoyed working with. You have been so helpful and patient with me. I love your personality you have a great sense of humor. You have always kept me on top of things, as well as giving me good advice. I have found you to be a good friend as well as a good publisher. May God continue to bless you!

Printed in the United States
50292LVS00006B/312